I0418820

Last Songs & True Magic

JOE LEIBOVICH

ENRAGED FEZ PUBLICATIONS/MEMPHIS, TN

Library of Congress Control Number: 2021917092

ISBN-13: 978-1-7377834-0-4

Titles by Joe Leibovich

Too Fat for Europe

DEDICATION

To my mother who has always believed in me and in creativity. And to my daughter, M, who I believe in even more.

CONTENTS

ACKNOWLEDGMENT

Thank you to anyone and everyone who has ever indulged my creative efforts in any capacity. I've had a lot of people willing to work with me in comedy, improv, writing, and podcasting over the years. It's meant a lot to me that so many talented and good people have been willing to join in with my nonsense. You all have done more for me than you will ever realize. Thank you especially to Christiana, who has tolerated, encouraged, and cajoled me to keep my creative side active and alive. I am far luckier than I have any right to be.

Foreword

Look, I'll be honest. This book is a bit of a mess.

I say that knowing a few things. The first is that I am simply awful at marketing my writing. My publicist would almost certainly tell me to start positive. But I don't have a publicist, so there you are and here we are.

The second thing I am aware of is that if this book gets any negative reviews, the critics will almost certainly quote the second sentence of this forward and declare that it is the one thing I got right in this collection. I accept this risk, and will try to graciously accept that judgment, which I hope is not inevitable.

This book is a collection of different genres and formats. There's a novella at the heart of this collection that lends its name to part of the title of the collection. There are some short pieces that are, I hope, entertaining and amusing. Many of these started out as items for The Howling Monkey Radio Network blog (and its predecessors).[1] There are also a bunch of short stories in here, most of which were born from flash fiction contests.

The flash fiction entries were confined to one-thousand words and had specific prompts. I've expanded all these stories, and in some cases eliminated or changed the prompted items from the final version.

---

[1] **www.howlingmonkeyradio.com**. In addition to written pieces, you'll find several podcasts. End of shameless plug.

The bookend stories, *Bones & Longe's Last Song* and *The Equinox Pattern,* were both stories written for the same prompts – horror/a recording studio/a highlighter. I wrote *Bones & Longe* first, and decided it wasn't even arguably scary. *The Equinox Pattern* fit the genre better, and it's the one that ended up as a submission. Both stories are here, expanded well beyond their initial one-thousand word limits (but hopefully not by so much as to be unnecessarily long). Neither story has a highlighter anymore.

These pieces are all over the map. There's humor stories and not so cleverly disguised lists. There's action. There's horror. There's even a rom-com in the mix. So, I apologize in advance if this collection gives you whiplash, vertigo, or any other malady.

The longest story in this collection is *True Magic,* which is a full-on novella. This one did not start with a contest or online. This one began with a germ of an idea in high school, which was more years ago than is rational to believe at this point. The original concept involved magic and bouillon cubes. I have no idea if those even still exist. When I came up with the idea, they were these cubes of compressed powdered soup stock wrapped in blue or red foil. The wrapper color indicated whether they were chicken or beef. I don't recall other flavors, but for some reason at the time I thought there was nothing funnier than bouillon cubes. It makes no sense, and no one around me shared this belief. As it stands, bouillon cubes may have, appropriately enough, formed the base for this story. But they are nowhere to be found in the final dish.

There probably should be something like a trigger warning for a few of these stories. Because there are many types of tales in this book, it seems only fair to alert readers about a couple of stories. Slight spoilers are somewhat unavoidable when you make these warnings, so if you don't need the warnings, skip the next paragraph.

Bisbee Abstract is violent. *The Equinox Pattern* is my attempt at horror, and it is violent and bloody. *Bones & Longe's Last Song* has some violence as well. There's some other violence in here, but I don't think that any of it likely needs to be highlighted, unless you are concerned about fairly mild curse words here and there. Otherwise, I don't think there's much that needs warning signs. Unless the mention of ghosts gets to you. There are a surprising number of ghosts in here, but most of them aren't particularly scary.

Thank you for taking the time to read this book and these stories. It means a lot to me. I sincerely hope you find something in here that makes your day a little better. If I can accomplish that, then I'll feel like I've done alright.

Bones and Longe's Last Song

Video didn't kill the radio star. It just put her on life support. The internet is what pulled the plug, and the music business as it had once been is deader than disco. The effects of online music rippled through the industry, making it harder for everyone to make a living off music, from artists to recording studios, and all the way up to the labels.

Delta Sounds was a small studio in the basement of a non-descript brick building in midtown Memphis, Tennessee. Alan "Bones" Baer built the studio in the 1970's. It boomed in the 80's and 90's, and started to sputter when the odometer clicked over to 2000.

People in the industry knew that Bones was an amazing producer. He could work the board like a surgeon, and he had over twenty framed gold records hanging on his studio walls. Bones was a big man, whether you measured his height or waistline. Every time he worked the board, he'd fire up a cigar ("It's not an expensive one, but it sure ain't cheap.") and work his magic. When he was on a streak, he'd sit at the board all night and well past sunrise. His wife, Theresa, helped with the books and business side, keeping Bones' artistic side in check as needed so that actual checks didn't bounce.

Bones could have moved to LA or Nashville and done well. But he liked being his own boss, and he liked his home. "I'd rather be a big damn fish in a small but respectable pond than a guppy in a corporate cesspool," he'd say from time to time.

Delta Sounds had three studios. When everything went digital, Bones reluctantly invested in computers and software, but he kept Studio A frozen in analog time. That was the only control room he'd personally work in. Bones would sit in an old desk chair, light a cigar, and help create some amazing music.

In 2003, Bones ran the board for the last time.

Jack Longe had worked with Bones on several projects over the years. He had been called "the New Dylan" in the 80's, but largely forgotten a decade later. The man could write, and he was a gifted acoustic guitarist. By the late 90's, Jack was on the skids professionally and personally. He'd lost his wife, his house, and, many said he'd lost his talent. He released his last album in 1997, which is about how many copies it sold.

One night in May 2003, Jack called Bones. In a slurred voice, Jack said, "Bones, I need to record. I've got my best song inside me. Help me get it out."

Jack arrived at Delta Sounds the next night. The neighborhood had seen better days, but so had Jack. He was shaky. Bones looked at him and said "Jack, buddy. I don't want to waste your money or my time."

"Just let me play, Bones. Then you can tell me if it's worth the time."

Bones agreed and led Jack through the glass front door to the stairway leading down to the studios. He closed the door, forgetting to lock it before leading Jack down to Studio A. Bones sat in his creaking black leather office chair by the board, as Jack set down his guitar case. Jack pulled out his old Martin and put the guitar's green strap over his shoulder. Jack pulled a sheet of paper out of the case, and with shaky hands, he put it on the wooden coffee table in front of a faded leather couch that was on the back wall of the control room.

Jack took a deep breath, and started to play and sing. Bones had never seen Jack play so well. Jack's fingers teased a sense of genuine longing and regret from the guitar, while his deep gravelly voice carried words that were powerful, sad, and beautiful. In less than four minutes, Jack Longe captured the essence of a lifetime of regret and missed opportunities.

When Jack finished, he looked up with eyes that contained seemingly infinite sorrow. Bones took a deep breath and said, "Buddy, that's the finest song I have ever heard."

Jack wiped a tear from his eye. "Bones, I can't pay you for studio time."

"Just get your ass into the live room, Jack. We're recording this now."

Jack opened the door between the control room and the live room, and walked into the familiar space, shutting the door behind him. Jack pulled up a wooden stool to a mic stand in the middle of the space. Bones set up the board and lit a cigar. He started the reel-to-reel tape deck and said, "Ready when you are, son."

As the reels started to spin, the control room door burst open. A young man with a gun and an addiction stormed into the room. Bones looked up from the board, and started talking to the man in a slow calm voice. "Friend, you don't need the gun. I'll...."

"Shut up!"

"No problem," Bones said. "You want my money? I'll give it to you, no worries."

Bones reached slowly to get his wallet, and the man panicked. His hand jerked and he shot Bones in the chest twice, killing him in a literal heartbeat. Bones dropped his cigar on the floor where it scorched a small spot in the carpet. The young man looked through the glass into the live room and saw Jack looking back at him with wet, gray eyes. The man with the gun opened the door and shot Jack Longe in the stomach. The singer collapsed and fell off the stool. The Martin was unharmed. Jack was dead.

The man took $83 in cash and some pills he found in Jack's pocket, and ran out of the studio, leaving the guitar clutched in Jack's hands. The reel-to-reel kept rolling.

Funeral services for Bones Baer attracted music heavyweights from around the country, and his death warranted a full page memorial piece in *Rolling Stone* the following month. Jack got a paragraph. The local news in Memphis used the incident as a catalyst to run a series of stories about the rise of crime and the decline of the city's once vibrant music business.

The police never found the kid that killed Jack and Bones, but he died less than a year later when he got squirrely during a drug deal.

Delta Sounds stayed open. Theresa figured it was paid for, and didn't have any employees. Overhead was low. Even so, the studio never made much money after the murders. People rented time and provided their own engineers, usually one of the other people in the band. It was enough to keep the doors open, but mainly just gave Theresa something of her husband to hold onto.

***

Eight years later, a college junior named Andy Hill rented studio time. He was studying music production at Middle Tennessee State University near Nashville, and played acoustic guitar. Most people who knew the name Jack Longe had heard the name because of the infamous "death tape." After Bones and Jack were gunned down, someone got hold of the reel-to-reel that recorded the killing. Ultimately a copy got uploaded, and it became one of those gruesome things that draw attention for a few weeks, and leads to debates as to whether it's an actual recorded death or if the story behind the thing is just apocryphal.

Andy had, of course, heard the recording. But, it was not how he first learned about Jack Longe and Bones. Andy had studied Jack since he first heard one of his early albums during high school. That record inspired Andy to pick up a guitar, and Andy's songwriting was heavily influenced by Jack Longe. Andy read everything he could get his hands on about the man, and by the time he was in college he knew as much about Longe and Bones as anybody who had never met them could.

Andy earned some money from his coffee shop gigs and part time jobs, and saved up enough to travel to Memphis during spring break and rent studio time at Delta Sounds so he could cut some demos surrounded by Jack's vibes. Theresa met him the night he arrived and gave him the keys to the building. "No one else is booked tonight, son, so you've got run of the place. You'll probably want to use Studio B. It's got a computer set up with Pro Tools and all that shit. Studio C's got some technical problems that I don't understand and that aren't worth dealing with."

"Can I look at, um," Andy started.

"Yeah. Knock yourself out, kid," Theresa said with a sad smile. "The place is yours for the night. Hell, you can stay 'til after lunch tomorrow. We got someone else booked then. But, listen, just keep the main door locked, okay?"

Andy said he would and thanked her. He took his guitar case down the stairs where there were two open doors. A faded, painted sign on the wall pointed to the right for Studios B and C, and to the left for Studio A. Studio B and C were on opposite sides of the hall, just past a small kitchen with a microwave, fridge and coffee maker. Andy went to Studio B and set his things down. After he situated his bag and guitar in the control room, he walked back out past the kitchen to the main hall.

He wanted to see the studio where Longe and Bones had recorded over the years and where they died. Andy walked through the door leading to Studio A. The walls were wood paneled, and the area was dimly lit. A closed office door was immediately to his right, and there were a couple of other closed doors. On the left wall was an open door with "Studio A" painted above it in black letters.

Andy walked to the studio and looked at the pictures on the wall. The gold records that had once hung there were long gone. The pictures were mostly local bands that had released an album or two, sprinkled with a few that had done a little better. Andy stopped at a photo of a thin man in a denim jacket. Andy looked at the intense gray eyes staring back at him from the photo. There was a sadness in them that Andy could feel. He'd seen that picture of Jack Longe hundreds of times before, but there was something about seeing it here that got to him.

Andy walked into the Studio A control room, and was hit with a wave of emotion. The room looked like a poorly maintained exhibit in a museum. A massive control board with banks of faders was on the wall opposite the door he'd come in. In front of it was a large window looking into the live room. An old reel-to-reel deck and other gear was on the wall opposite the panel next to the faded leather couch. In front of the couch was a wooden coffee table, and a banged-up metal file cabinet was next to the control panel. Two beat up black leather office chairs were behind the control panel. A large, round black enamel ashtray sat on the right-hand corner of the panel. The room's carpeting looked ancient, and Andy saw it had numerous burn marks, including one near the control board.

Andy opened the door to the live room, and walked in. He flicked on three switches, each turning on bright overhead lighting over sections of the room. It was a large space with walls covered in black foam acoustic panels. The foam deadened sound and created a sensation of stillness in the room that Andy could almost feel. A banged-up drum kit set up behind isolation panels sat in the rear corner, and in the middle of the room was a wooden stool in front of a mic stand. A Shure was plugged into an XLR cable that snaked to a hook up. A black metal music stand was beside the stool. The room was otherwise empty.

Andy walked across the dirty beige carpeting to the stool. He stood in the spot where he assumed Jack Longe had been gunned down. He thought he could see faded blood stains in the carpet, but realized it could just as easily be spilt coffee or even just ground in dirt. Standing there, looking at the control room brought a lump to Andy's throat. He didn't cry, but it was a close thing.

Andy sat on the stool and tapped the microphone. It was dead. Andy breathed in the control room's air. This was the spot that Jack Longe had recorded the songs that had gotten Andy through high school and had made him want to create. It was also the spot where Jack Longe had died.

Andy sat for a few minutes before he got up and walked back to the cleaner, more modern Studio B and got to work.

Three hours later, Andy heard what sounded like knocking on a door from somewhere in the building. He left the studio and walked up the stairs to the Delta Sounds main entrance. It was locked and no one was there. He heard the banging again from downstairs. When he got downstairs he heard the noise coming from his left. From where Studio A was.

Andy walked into the Studio A control room. The sound was coming from the middle drawer of the green metal filing cabinet. Andy thought that maybe a critter had gotten trapped in there somehow. He approached the cabinet, and slowly opened the drawer, readying himself to deal with whatever animal he might encounter. There was no rat or raccoon inside the drawer. The only thing inside was a single piece of faded paper ripped from a spiral notebook.

Andy looked at the sheet with handwritten lyrics. He recognized the writing, which he had seen many times over the years in books. Despite his firm belief that he was looking at something in Jack Longe's handwriting, he told himself that couldn't be right. The lyrics certainly weren't to any of Longe's tunes that Andy knew, and he knew them all. Written on the bottom was simply "5/9/03". The lyrics were amazing, but Andy had no idea what the tune was supposed to be.

As he finished reading the page, the center light in the live room turned on, and the control board hummed to life. The door between the control room and the live room opened. Without thinking about it, Andy walked in. He moved from the shadows and into the middle of the room, which was bathed in the overhead light. On the floor next to a wooden stool was an open guitar case with an old acoustic Martin inside. The case and guitar had not been there a few hours earlier. Andy, acting without thought, picked up the guitar and slung the green strap over his shoulder. He put his hand around the neck of the Martin, and it felt warm and somehow right.

The door to the live room closed slowly. Andy looked through the window into the control room and saw the reel-to-reel come to life. He breathed slowly, feeling the deadened air blanketing him. In the dim light of the control room he thought he saw, or at least sensed, that the faders on the board were moving. A faint orange glow appeared in the booth, just behind and in the center of the board. The air felt thick and smoky.

Out of the corner of his eye, he thought he saw a shadow move beside him. Andy set the paper on the music stand, and he saw the shadow again. He closed his eyes, and when he opened them, he knew the song.

He heard a voice say, "Ready when you are, son."

Andy took a breath, looked at the lyric sheet and played better than he had ever played before. His fingers didn't miss a chord, and his voice was filled with more emotion than he'd ever been able to summon in his life. What he sang was strong and sad. The song was filled with regret and love and loss and yearning. He sweated as he pushed his voice to meet every nuance of the lyrics.

Three minutes and twenty-five seconds after he started, Andy was finished, and the reel-to-reel clicked to a stop. He was shaking. He looked up from the lyric sheet and focused his teary eyes on the control booth. He saw two figures standing there. He couldn't make out any of their features. Andy wiped his eyes, and they were gone. The air was clear. Andy took the guitar off his shoulder and set it back in the case along with the lyric sheet.

Andy picked up the case and took it into the control room. He rewound the reel-to-reel and took the full plastic reel off the deck. Andy took it and the guitar case with him. As he left studio, he passed Jack Longe's picture on the wall. The eyes looking back at him didn't seem as sad as they had before.

***

A month later, Andy sent out copies of a CD with the material he had cut at Delta Sounds. A producer with an indie label in Nashville that received one of the copies had worked with both Jack and Bones, and he was floored by the demo. He brought Andy in to record some other tracks, and the label published Andy's debut album several months later.

Most critics said all the tracks were strong, but there was almost universal agreement that one song stood out above the others. A respected music writer went so far as to call it one of the best acoustic songs of the last thirty years, and possibly the best ever. Andy titled the track *Bones and Longe's Last Song*. He credited Jack as the writer, and donated his share of the royalties to that song to a trust he set up with Theresa to keep Delta Sounds open. The foundation provided education to music students, and subsidized studio time for artists who would not otherwise be able to afford it.

The gear in Studio A was kept as it had been, with just enough maintenance to keep it going as a working studio. Artists didn't use Studio A much. Studio B and the now fully functional Studio C were equipped with the latest gear and digital tools. From time to time someone used A out of a sense of nostalgia for the analog process. The appeal of old school methods made sense in an era when vinyl and turntables were staging a ferocious comeback.

Between the students learning and the working musicians who want to soak in the atmosphere and hope it infuses their work, Delta Sounds is busier than it has ever been. Jack Longe's songs are steadily streamed as a new generation discovers him, thanks in large part to *Bones and Longe's Last Song*.

Now when people record in Studio A, they say something about it makes the mix sweeter and the lyrics sharper. No one can put their finger on what it is, but there's just something about Studio A. Some argue that the acoustics in the live room are exactly right. Others claim there's a quality to the old board that tweaks the sound in a way that modern mixers cannot.

But the reality of it is something different. The energy of Bones and Longe permeate the space, and their final recording still lingers in the air of Studio A. And, when you get right down to it, the truth is last songs never really die.

Closing Time Bar Inspection Report

To: Mr. T. Waits
From: Frank Wild, Department of Inspection

The recent inspection of your establishment, the Rain Dog Bar and Grill, conducted near closing time, has brought to light several unusual deficiencies. You must immediately remedy the following violations if you want to avoid closure and/or fines that could leave you deep, down in the hole:

1. The piano appears to be intoxicated.

2. Men's neck apparel suffers from narcolepsy, which is alarming if nothing else.

3. Despite the fact that the venue promotes live music, the band is not present, and is rumored to have fled to New York for reasons unknown.

4. The jukebox is emitting fluids. This is a clear safety concern as it creates unsafe walking surfaces for the public and staff.

5. The carpeting is dangerously thick and in need of trimming.

6. The house lighting gives the illusion that convicts are escaping from a federal penitentiary, which is disconcerting at best.

7.The telephone will not dispense cigarettes, which is a significant inconvenience for patrons.

8. The balcony is investigating ways of netting large profits. This raises the specter of fraud, which is unacceptable.

9. Menus are all dangerously cold to the touch, leading to the real possibility of frostbite or more significant injury.

10. It is difficult to locate serving staff, even when utilizing a Geiger counter. (Note: This is actually a positive notation, as it indicates employees are not radioactive as they were rumored to be).

11. Members of the serving staff, when located, are notably ill-tempered.

12. The lighting technician does not have adequate depth perception, and is arguably totally blind. This creates a potential fire and/or injury hazard for patrons and staff who pass underneath overhead fixtures.

13. The on-call piano tuner is hard of hearing, and has brought unauthorized personnel to the area (namely his mother). This impacts both the quality of the entertainment on offer as well as potentially creating a violation of the venue's maximum capacity.

14. The bouncer is morbidly obese.

15. Menu item "Cream Puff Casper Milk Toast" makes no sense.

16. The owner has the functional intellectual capacity of a fence post. No offense is intended by this, but it does raise concerns about his ability to manage the operation in a safe and ethical manner.

17. The venue box office is spilling fluids onto the ground. This, combined with the issue with the jukebox, creates an even more serious slipping hazard.

18. Bar stools are routinely combusting into flames. The concern here is obvious.

19. Newspapers provided at bar are not accurate.

20. There is a dearth of ashtrays, which may be connected to the flaming bar stool issue.

21. And, once again, it bears noting that the piano, somehow, appears to be intoxicated.

This inspector feels compelled to note that he did not partake any intoxicants during the inspection, and is not currently under the influence of any impairing substances. This is more than can be said for one patron, a professional jockey, who was observed being overserved bourbon on the evening of the inspection.

Once these deficiencies are cured, we will be able to provide a passing grade to your establishment.

***

Follow up note: Owner has reportedly sailed to Singapore and is unavailable to remedy the issues. He has referenced all further inquiries to "A. Tawny Moor," his attorney.

Overnight Crossing

"LaGuardia's been a crap shoot for, what, two years now," Matt Cox said, lighting a cigarette and taking a drag. "The day Reagan fired the controllers was the day our job became a giant pain in the ass."

Co-pilot Steve Lewis had heard the sermon before, but Cox was not one to let a captive audience go to waste, and a night crossing of the Atlantic provided plenty of time for pontification. Steve had tried several avoidance strategies. The most effective was to make non-committal grunts combined with looking out the cockpit window. Sometimes the thought of leaping from the 747 with or without a parachute and taking his chances at sea had some appeal, but ultimately that wasn't practical. So, Steve nodded, tuning out Cox's diatribe on the White House's handling of the PATCO strike. Steve felt sorry for Cox's wife, Mary. She couldn't easily escape either.

Cox wound down, "Screw it, we've got four hours before we have to worry about it. Hopefully someone in the tower knows what the hell they are doing."

Cox started flying commercially after he got back from Vietnam. Steve was younger, and although he did a stint in the Navy, he didn't see combat. Cox made it a point of reminding Steve of this almost as regularly as he opined on the President.

Cindy Murray, the head stewardess, opened the cockpit door and wheeled in a cart.

"You guys are in luck," Cindy said. "We've got chicken or chicken tonight. I recommend chicken."

"Sounds good, Cindy. You should join us for a romantic dinner under the stars," Cox said, pointing to the dark night sky outside the windows.

"Now, Captain, what would your wife say? I doubt she'd approve."

"You'd be surprised what she approves of, right, Steve?" Cox asked with a hash edge.

"Chicken sounds good," Steve said, looking out the window.

Cindy passed them dinner trays, and asked what they wanted to drink.

"I'll take a Coke with ice," Cox said, while Steve requested water.

Cindy handed them their drinks and left the cockpit.

"She likes you," Cox said. "She's closer to your age than some of the women you've been sleeping with."

Steve began to eat his meal in silence.

Cox popped open his Coke and poured it into the glass. The ice cracked. Cox took a drink, sucking in an ice cube, rolling it around in his mouth. He took a bite – too big of one – of the chicken.

"It's not ..." Steve began to say, as the jet plunged. Screams and crashes erupted on the other side of the cockpit door. The plane had encountered an invisible and violent downdraft.

Steve grabbed the stick, but the yoke fought him. "Damnit, Cox, pull!" Steve shouted, turning to look at the captain, who was slumped backwards in his chair, his hands at his throat.

Steve couldn't help Cox. Both hands were on the yoke, and he was straining against it so hard that he was sweating. Red lights flashed and a loud buzzer competed with Steve's screams to Cox.

The altimeter spun as the 747 plummeted towards the Atlantic like a stone.

A blue flash filled the cockpit. The altimeter slowed, then stopped. The cacophony that filled the flight deck was replaced with deafening silence. Tendrils of frost crisscrossed the inside of the cockpit window.

Steve felt cold and sluggish, and the controls were frozen. He slowly turned his head to see that Cox's hands had fallen to his side, and he was not moving. The captain was dead.

The blue light coalesced behind Cox into a dully glowing blue shape that was vaguely human.

Steve's breath was visible in the cold air.

"I survived firefights in 'Nam only to get taken out by airline chicken. How dumb is that?" Cox's voice said from the shape.

"What ..." Steve said.

"Choked when we took the dive. Can you believe that?"

Steve sat dumbstruck.

"I should have opened with 'Boo!' or something," Cox said. "I'm new to this. Well, you know. You were there. You *are* there."

"You're..." Steve started.

"Dead. I'm dead. I guess I'm a ghost."

Steve didn't reply.

"It's weird. I feel like I've been dead for years. Time's all screwed up wherever I am. Here's the thing, I can't move into the light. That's real, by the way. Big tunnel of beautiful light. But I can't move into it."

"Wh...why?" Steve asked.

"Unfinished business. I'm stuck in this cockpit until I resolve that. Which means I may be stuck haunting a plane wreck at the bottom of the Atlantic for eternity. That's a bum deal."

Steve didn't speak.

"Steve. Let's talk about Mary."

"Your wife?"

"That's the one. I know about you two."

"You've got it wrong," Steve said, forgetting he was arguing with a ghost. "There's nothing going on."

"I know. You haven't slept with her, not yet. But it's going to happen sooner or later."

"That's not true!"

"Relax," Cox said. "A few minutes ago, it was a problem. Now, well, I have a different perspective. I need you to promise me you'll look after her. You're a good guy. She likes you. Just makes sure she's okay."

Steve nodded.

"Good. Tell her I love her. God knows I should have told her that more. Tell her I'm not mad and I just need her to be happy. Can you do that?"

"Yes," Steve said.

"I think that takes care of it then. Man, I could use a smoke. Be good to yourself and our Mary, ok?"

"I will."

The shape condensed into a blue ball. The buzzer and screams returned, and the cabin temperature returned to normal. The altimeter resumed spinning.

The energy ball shot into the control panel in front of Steve with a crackle, and the yoke moved easily in Steve's hands. The 747 levelled off and began to climb.

The plane was safe.

Steve looked over to Cox's body, and called in Cindy. She handled the situation professionally, retrieving a physician who was in first class. The doctor confirmed that Cox was deceased. He promised he would not tell his fellow passengers what the situation was.

After the doctor and Cindy left the cabin, Steve got on the intercom and reassured the passengers that they had just hit a patch of turbulence, but that the situation was under control.

"Everything is going to be okay," he said over the intercom. "It's going to be fine."

LaGuardia and Mary were just over three hours away. Steve looked over at Cox, and thought to himself that he hoped the guys in the tower knew what the hell they were doing.

Questions Raised by *Willy Wonka*

I recently showed *Willy Wonka & The Chocolate Factory* (the 1971 Gene Wilder version) to my daughter, as she had never seen it before. I had not seen the movie in a very long time, and this viewing raised a lot of questions.

1. Where is this movie set? It looks like it was shot in a German village populated by people with British accents. Except for Charlie's family and Willy Wonka, who seem to be American. Is this a place like the Village from *The Prisoner*, and everyone is a former spy or the families of former spies? Maybe that's what happened to Charlie's father. He was killed doing spy stuff. Maybe he was James Bond or something. Never mind. This whole theory is dumb, but, still, where is this movie set?

2. That guy who sings "The Candy Man" comes off as a little weird, right?

3. Why is there some sinister character hanging around the chocolate factory at all hours dispensing creepy exposition to children?

4. For that matter, why is Charlie allowed to roam the streets at night? His family is not concerned for his safety. Maybe that's just how spy families are.

5. Charlie's grandparents – all four of them – are bedridden, and have been for decades. They all share a

single bed in the middle of the living room. Meanwhile, Charlie has his own room and bed. The whole thing seems odd.

6. Don't even get me started on that malingering Grandpa Joe. What a jerk he is!

7. Charlie's teacher is not good at his job at all.

8. So this whole contest is purportedly to award a tour of a factory and a lifetime supply of chocolate. So why are people going so berserk over it? I mean, the amount of money Mr. Salt spent on the chocolate to find the ticket could have probably been set aside for all the family's chocolate needs forever.

9. The amount of time it takes from the start of the movie until they get to the factory tour is egregious. That "Cheer Up, Charlie" song alone seems to last an hour. And then there's the excruciatingly long sequence of Charlie running home after he wins the ticket. Seriously, watch that again sometime. It's like the *Forrest Gump* running montage.

10. Who set up the chairs and red carpet outside the factory for the big day? Wouldn't someone have seen that happening?

11. The Oompa Loompas are moralistic about very strange things. Gluttony, fine. It's a seven-deadly sin and all. And spoiled kids, sure, I can see that. But they seem a little high and mighty about gum chewing and watching television. Also, I can accept that maybe Oompa Loompa are musical improvisers on the level of Wayne Brady who can come up with songs on the spot about various moral lessons. But when did they choreograph their dances? Seems a little too polished to not have been pre-planned.

12. Let's talk about the musical numbers in general. They are oddly inconsistent. Why does anyone, other than the Oompa Loompas, break into song. There's the sad song by mom. There's the song Grandpa Joe sings when he gets out of bed (which he clearly could have done at any time...jerk), Bill the weird candy seller sings a song, Willy Wonka sings an oddly melancholy song that, by all rights should be a happy one (why is he so sad singing "Pure Imagination"?), and then Veruca sings one while having a tantrum. That's basically it. It's a musical that's not really committed to being a musical. I don't think Charlie, the protagonist, even sings one.

13. Why does Wonka keep making vaguely risqué statements to Veruca Salt's dad? Were they in a fraternal lodge together or something?

14. Did the kids, overall, really do anything that bad? Veruca, yes. She was awful. But all Augustus Gloop did was drink chocolate after specifically being told – by Willy Wonka himself, no less – that everything in the room was edible. Then Wonka basically pushed him in the river. Violet chewed some gum after being mildly told that it wasn't ready, and Mike TeeVee just got excited about teleportation technology, because, well, it's freakin' teleportation technology. For their "crimes" they were almost drowned, inflated to possibly fatal proportions, and shrunk to the size of a mouse. Seems harsh, really.

15. Which brings us to Charlie. What he did was as bad or worse than what most of the kids did. He explicitly disobeyed an order from Wonka, but he didn't suffer any weird fate. Sure, he almost got chopped up by a fan, but nothing actually happened to him. At the end, he was given the Gobstopper morality test and passed. Why did he get that chance and none of the other kids

did? Wonka was being blatantly unfair with this.

16. Are the Oompa Loompas covered by any collective bargaining agreement? In any case, are they being paid at all? Is there an on-site physician? How are worker's compensation claims – of which there would likely be many based on the horrifically unsafe conditions at the plant – handled?

17. The facility seems to be run in a very inefficient and slipshod manner, yet Wonka chocolates are shipped worldwide. Who is handling logistics?

18. For that matter, how does the product get out of the plant and into the distribution chain? No one goes in and no one comes out, according to the expository creepy figure. How does the product get to stores then?

19. Is it even legal for a child to run a chocolate factory?

20. I hope Charlie makes Grandpa Joe do some honest work at the plant after they move in. That guy has been feigning a disability for decades. He could have helped out the family for years and made enough money to buy his own damn tobacco.

21. I bet Charlie's mom is quietly stewing over how much Charlie seems to like Grandpa Joe over her, when she does everything for the family. Charlie should have at least asked her if she wanted to go on the factory tour. But he didn't. I feel this deserves an Oompa Loompa song.

22. What was the point of the elevator shooting out of the building and destroying the roof? That won't be a cheap fix. Wonka left Charlie with an immediate major expenditure.

23. Will Charlie inherit the civil liability from the things that happened to the kids who went on the tour? Oh sure, the kids signed a waiver, but they are minors

and there's no way those agreements are enforceable. Charlie needs to find a good lawyer. Or barrister. Or burgermeister. Or whatever is appropriate in their ill-defined country.

24. How come no childless adults found a golden ticket? I'd have been amused if some 45-year-old guy named Brad found one and just showed up by himself for the tour.

25. Why did that Tim Burton thing happen after this?

Love and Pancakes at the Top of the World

I have been to Mount Everest three times, but never to the top. Bad weather scrubbed my first attempt. A kidney stone did it next. I blame the pancake for the third time.

Just getting to the base of Mount Everest is an ordeal. There are permits to obtain, tour companies to coordinate, and an enormous amount of money to part with. If you want to follow in Hillary and Norgay's footsteps along Everest's South Col route, you fly into Tribhuvan International Airport in Kathmandu. Then there's a horrifying flight to Lukla, which is on a mountain and has a strip of tarmac that is more driveway than runway. It's a wonder planes don't routinely smash into or slide off that mountain.

From Lukla you hike to base camp, which more by providence than design, gives you the chance to start your acclimation to the higher altitudes. Although I contract with a Sherpa group, I make this pre-trek journey alone. These days of solitude are immeasurably valuable. Well, not quite immeasurably. I could show you receipts, and you'd want to set me on fire.

The morning after arriving in Lukla, I set out with my backpack and headed for the Namche Bazaar, a village considered to be the gateway to Everest. After crossing a series of suspension bridges and making a long climb up a hill, I arrived at Namche Bazaar. Buildings with brightly colored roofs stacked on plateaus make up the village that serves as an outpost for Everest pilgrims.

Upon arrival, I made my way the hotel where I would be staying for a few nights as I took mini-treks, all as part of the acclimation process. Dorje, a friendly Sherpa in his late sixties, owned the hotel. His English is excellent, and he seems to enjoy speaking with travelers at the hotel bar at night.

Dorje greeted me when I made it to the hotel. He acted like we were old friends, and I'd like to think he remembered me from my past visits due to my undeniable charm. But, I must admit the fact that my face has been plastered on newspapers, magazines, and every news site on the internet for the better part of a decade may have also been a factor.

I called it a night early, and made a half-day trek the next day. That night, I sat in the hotel's bar. It was packed as it was every evening during the short climbing season. A dark-haired woman in her early 30's sat next to me and ordered a Jameson. Dorje told her he didn't have any, but could provide a substitute.

"There's actually an Irish pub nearby," I said.

The woman was wearing a black sweater and a dark green down vest, a look she pulled off remarkably well. She looked at me with a thin smile.

"An Irish pub," she said. "You mean the one that everyone knows about?"

"I guess I'm mountainsplaining," I said, proud of myself. I extended my hand. "I'm Richard."

Dorje returned with her drink.

"I know who you are. You killed my father," she said, walking away, her substitute Irish whisky in hand.

I guess that murder slipped my mind.

***

After a few days, I left Namche for Everest's southern base camp. The hike to the camp takes you through other villages and past numerous strings of multi-colored prayer flags rippling in the wind. The southern base camp is set on the rocky Khumbu Glacier at the foot of Everest at an altitude of nearly 18,000 feet. Once you make it there, you can claim you've climbed Mount Everest. Just not a lot of it.

I located the flag bearing the logo of the Sherpa company I had contracted with and found my tent. I dropped my pack inside the tent and then walked to the larger communal tent set up for the two-week acclimation period. These tent cities sprout like wild mushrooms at the base of Everest every year. Base camp is more than an overnight campout. You don't show up at the base and zip up Everest the same day. There are multiple rotations that involve increasingly long hikes to a series of camps and back. Some of the treks involve an overnight stay at a secondary camp. This process gets your body used to the altitude, and hopefully keeps the mountain from killing you.

Several climbers were inside the relative warmth of the large tent. "Are you following me?" the woman from Namche asked as I entered.

I sat in a camp chair beside her. "I'm sorry about the loss of your father," I said.

"He's not dead. You just fired him five years ago."

"Who's your father?"

"No one you know. He was an industrial engineer in your Boston facility."

"I'm sorry. But, you know I probably didn't have anything to do with that, right?"

"I know, but it felt good to call you a murderer. On principle. I'm Lisa Callan," she said, extending her hand. "If we're going to climb this mountain I need to be cordial, but I don't have to like you."

"I barely do myself," I said, shaking her hand. She smiled.

The next day, the group climbed for a couple of hours and descended. On the way down, I stopped to admire the scenery and catch my breath. Lisa had the same idea.

"It's amazing, isn't it?" I asked. "Is this your first attempt?"

"It is. Is this where you ask how I can afford this? Just because you fired my dad doesn't mean I don't have a good job."

"I ..."

"It's not as good as yours," she interrupted. "But it's 'Climb Everest once' good."

"I had you pegged as making 'Mount Hood' money at least."

She laughed, and we returned to camp.

Over the next several days, we talked, mainly when we were back at base camp. I learned she practiced domestic law in Boston, and got divorced herself a couple of years earlier. I pointed out the irony, but she said my grasp on that term was as tenuous as Alanis Morissette's.

She told me her father was fired because of an argument with he had with a V.P. "It was probably his fault. He can be abrasive."

"Family trait?" I asked, and she nudged my shoulder with hers. I felt like I had been struck by a bolt of lightning.

We began our first rotation about a week after we arrived. We scaled the Icefall, with its ladders crossing deadly chasms, before reaching the flat icy spot where our crew set up Camp 1. We would stay there before returning to base the next morning. Exhausted, Lisa and I stood at the edge of camp and watched thin clouds that fluttered like flags from Everest's white peak. We kissed. I knew then I never wanted to kiss anyone else.

We grew closer, spending as much time together as we could. Our budding romance was chaste but we both knew there was something real and strong between us. We were flirting with making plans after we returned from the top of the world.

About a week before we were to start our summit attempt, the lead guide let us know we would have to start two days early due to weather issues. The season was narrowing. We were excited and nervous that our climb was that much closer. The combination of that and our newfound relationship made Lisa and me giddy. We found ourselves acting like school kids, and it felt good.

Two days before the summit attempt, our crew made breakfast including rikikur, flour and potato creations commonly called Sherpa pancakes.

I grabbed one on the way out of the communal tent. I asked Lisa if she wanted it, playfully tossing it to her. She stepped back to catch it, and slipped on loose rocks and Khumbu ice. Her leg twisted and she fell hard. I could swear I heard a crack.

I helped Lisa to the medic's tent to see the camp physician. She confirmed that Lisa's leg was broken and that there was no way she would be making an ascent this season. People break bones on Everest routinely, but this had to be the mountain's first pancake related injury.

We arranged for an airlift to Kathmandu. Lisa insisted I continue the climb, claiming that Everest has a three strikes rule. "It's harsh, but fair," she said with a dry chuckle. I tried to argue with her, but she wouldn't hear of it. She promised we would see each other after I got home. We both knew this probably was not true, and that this was one of those little lies people tell each other to make things easier.

I nodded and told her I would wait with her until the helicopter arrived.

Two hours later, the helicopter arrived, and the crew loaded Lisa in. I put her backpack in beside her. I kissed her, and we looked into each other's eyes for what we knew was the last time.

But it wasn't.

I lowered a black folded seat bolted to the inside of the helicopter's frame and sat down. I gave the pilot a thumb's up, and he nodded. The medivac copter began to lift off. Lisa tried to protest, but I could see her smile. Both of us were crying.

Everest became smaller by the moment.

***

After a few days in Kathmandu, I arranged for a private jet to take us to Boston. Lisa's leg had a nasty spiral fracture, and she would need some time to recover. I decided I needed to spend a few weeks at the Boston facility – a decision that no one at the Boston facility agreed with or welcomed, no doubt. I did my best to take care of Lisa during her convalescence. The morning after we arrived in Boston, I offered her breakfast, which she agreed to if I did not try to foist pancakes on her. I agreed, and we compromised with waffles. One morning I made a call, and her father had a job offer the next day with my company. He declined, and told Lisa I was "a stinkbug." I like him.

That was six months ago. Our wedding is set for July. We haven't decided on our honeymoon spot yet, but we agree that it's going to be somewhere warm and flat. Everest can wait.

Because, you know, it's there.

Random Lines From That Noir Novel I Am Writing

I am nearly finished with my gritty, non-derivative detective novel, *The Game of Lies*. It will soon be available from some wisenheimer bookworm type. Here are some random lines from the novel to whet your appetite:

1. I woke up with the taste of bourbon on my tongue and the smell of gunpowder on my fingers. Both happen more often than is advisable.

2. Melanie Bollingham was the kind of dame that made you pray for rain, just so she'd be stuck there high and dry with you for just a few more hours 'til the storm passed.

3. The old man had money, and plenty, but he didn't seem interested in parting with any of it too quickly. That's the trick to money. You have it as long as you have it.

4. The pug took a swing at me, and hard. If his haymaker had connected, I'd have been dozing in the Grand Palooka Hotel for the night. Fortunately for me, he missed and I didn't, and he got to check in under the reservation that had been made for me.

5. "Take it easy, Jimmy," I said. "I got not beef with you, and you don't want one with me. So, let's all point our heaters at the ground and talk like civilized reprobates."

6. I found the girl right where Melanie said I would. But Melanie had left out one important fact. Her sister wasn't just trouble. Her sister was dead.

7. "A most unfortunate business," the old man said as he looked out towards the ocean. "No one blames you, of course, Mr. Stone. But, you won't blame me if I don't continue to retain your services. Or if I see to it that no one else does either."

8. It was never about the girl. It was always about the old man's money. And I had been set up like ten wooden pins ready to be bowled over to take the fall for his murder.

9. It was one gunshot. And one second. But both felt like more.

10. "This one's going to take some doing, Stone," Sgt. Connor said. "But, I've seen you wriggle your way out of worse. Just like the snake you are."

11. In the end, it was just another night. And in the morning, there'd be the familiar taste of bourbon and smell of gunpowder to remind me I'd just been played in another game of lies.

True Magic

"There is magic in this world," said the woodsman to his son. "If you see, truly see, an acorn grow into a tree, and that tree be turned to lumber, and that lumber be turned into a house, you cannot doubt that magic is real."
"But, that is boring," said the boy.
"And that is the nature of magic. True magic is boring. And that is why so few people bother to do it."

- An excerpt from the Austrian collection of tales *The Wisdom of the Woods*, author unknown.

All persons and events depicted in this story are fictional. Any resemblance to any person living or dead, and particularly those who are litigious, is strictly coincidental.

   If you find yourself among a group of magicians, it is not difficult to get them to discuss, *ad nauseum*, their art and its practitioners throughout history. Ask them, or don't, for surely, they will offer this information unprompted, who the greatest magician of all time is, and you will not get a consensus. You will get a Houdini or a Houdine. A Dai Vernon or a Ricky Jay. A Copperfield here, a Blackstone there. Some will vehemently argue that Penn & Teller belong at the top for their skill and their rock and roll popularization of the craft. Occasionally, someone will toss David Blaine or Criss Angel into the mix. Regardless of the choice, the practitioners will agree they have named great showmen who brought new technique to the art; they were good at selling the sizzle.

So, when you ask magicians who the best among them ever was, they will argue about the specifics of the who, but will invariably agree on the why as they give you a list of technically proficient performers who knew how to put on a good show.

But when you ask these same magicians, preferably after they have been into their cups – regular cups filled with whiskey and wine and not balls or flowers or doves – if there was ever anyone who came close to performing actual, honest to God magic, they will pause. And then they will quibble about religious figures and mythical figures. But once you get them past that, and if they will answer you, every single one of them will reluctantly admit that they know of only one person who ever performed actual magic.

His name was Jim Lane, and as far as anyone can tell, he is the only human being who ever lived who could perform feats of actual magic. The problem was that he wasn't particularly good at it. And it just wasn't that interesting.

Jim grew up in Memphis, Tennessee with a love of magic. Every Sunday morning, one of the local television stations aired a half-hour magic show. *Mel Hall's Magic Menagerie* had been on the air for years before Jim discovered it when he was six, and it stayed on the air until he was in his teens. Every Sunday that his family wasn't in church, which was most of them, young Jim would watch Mel Hall's routines and study his patter. The fact that Hall repeated both with great regularity made it easy.

For his ninth birthday, Jim's parents gave him a box full of plastic vases, "silk" scarves, wooden wands, a deck of cards and various other doodads. The words "Marvelous Magnifico's Instant Magic Show – 75 Tricks to Tantalize and Astound!" were emblazoned on the box in yellow letters printed on top of a red background made to look like velvet curtains.

Jim devoured the instructions, and practiced for hours on end. One month later, under the stage name of the Great TopDini, a name he gave himself after making a large construction paper top hat that accompanied a ratty green towel that served as a cape. Jim performed his first show for family, friends and neighbors, commanding a solid twenty-five cents per audience member. His take was a cool dollar fifty. The show was terrible, even if judged against other nine-year old prestidigitators. Jim's patter was wooden. He fumbled coins and scarves, and his sleight of hand was sleight at best. One trick bled into another. There was no pause for applause, which was clearly not warranted anyway.

Twelve minutes after it started, the Great TopDini's debut concluded to the polite, if insincere, applause of his paying customers. People want to be nice to kids, by and large.

By the time Jim was in high school, he was what was jeans manufacturers called "husky", and he existed in a state of constant dishevelment. Someone once said his shirt looked like a hand grenade went off inside of it because it was always untucked. Jim was forced to rely on his personality to get by, which was unfortunate, because Jim was an awkward lad. It is unfair to say Jim had a hard time making friends, because he didn't really try to do so. He was soft spoken, sometimes to the point of mumbling. He was not much of a joiner, but did participate in his high school's magic club. The club consisted of five students, four boys and one girl. Jim and three of the others were on the same echelon of social insecurity. One of the students, however, was handsome, charismatic, and assured to a degree that made up for the deficits in those categories possessed by the other members of the club. He was Marcus Wade, who was president of the high school magic club.

The club met at the Sorcerer's Table, which is what the club members called the cafeteria table where they ate lunch. Regular club meetings were daily at lunch. Special meetings convened weekly in the classroom of Ms. Gold, the math teacher who had been delegated responsibility for the club.

"Magicians," Marcus declared one day at the Sorcerers' Table. "The time has come for us to soar!"

"Levitation?" asked Stan Huang, one of the members.

"Not quite," said Marcus, flipping a tater tot into the air and casually catching it in his mouth. "I think it is time to put our talents on display. Fellow practitioners, we will perform our magic for the entire school!"

"When?" asked Jim, not looking up from the square piece of pizza that sat on his tray, tantalizing him with its perfect geometry and unidentifiable aroma.

"One month hence!" Marcus said with a flourish.

"No way!" said Allison Barnes, who went by Ally.

"We can't do that!" said Stan.

"Are you high?" asked Nick Parson, the final member of the club.

"Not as high as we all shall be!" declared Marcus.

"So, we are doing levitation?" Stan asked.

"Stan, while your enthusiasm for the art of levitation is, as always, appreciated, I do not think it is practical to focus on that discipline at this time," Marcus said. "We need sleight of hand and illusion! Some danger, maybe even derring-do! What say you?"

The other members muttered noncommittally while taking a sudden interest in their lunches. All but Jim.

"I'm in," he said.

And, one by one, the others agreed.

"Excellent!" said Marcus, slapping the palm of his hand on the Sorcerer's Table. "Now, first order of business. We really do need to come up with a name. The School Magic Club just does not have much panache."

"Well, I guess we have to go with the school's mascot in the name, right?" asked Ally. And no one could think of a compelling reason to disagree. So, for the next month, the Mystic Order of the Broncos met daily after school to practice and build a show.

Marcus was already adept at stage illusions. Nick was good with cards. Ally could juggle, which, while not technically magic, was magic adjacent. Stan was determined to put together a levitation routine. And Jim had some basic silk work and starter level routines. Cups and balls and magic linking rings. The kind of thing his nine-year-old self should have been able to do right out of Marvelous Magnifico's box.

After a month of practices on weekends and after school, the day of the show arrived. Ms. Gold talked to principal Haynes, to ask her permission to use the assembly hall for a lunchtime show. Principal Haynes agreed to let the club do a show in the auditorium, but declined to let them charge admission. She also refused to make the show compulsory. If students wanted to spend their lunch watching a magic show, they could. But nobody was paying for the privilege.

A week before the show, Marcus handed the group some yellow sheets of paper bearing the words, "Make Your Lunch Magical – Starring The Mystic Order of Broncos" and listing the date and time for the show. The flyer had a picture of a horse surrounded by cards and smoke. "Fellow wizards, take these notices and carry forth the word of our display of mystic magic! Let the populous know that next week they shall dine on illusion and wonder instead of tater tots and fish sticks for one magical 30-minute period!"

"Wait, are they going to let them eat lunch during the show?" asked Nick.

"Alas, no," Marcus said. "The rules forbid food and drink in the hall of miracles."

"Hall of miracles?" asked Jim.

"That's what the auditorium shall be called on show day!"

"That's cool," said Stan.

"That's dumb," said Nick.

"Your negativity shall not displace my zeal," Marcus said.

"If they can't eat, no one is going to come," Nick said. "This is stupid."

"Rain on another parade, Nick! This show will be the stuff of legends."

"This is stupid."

On show day, Nick was proven wrong. Despite his prediction that no one would attend the show, seven people did. The rest went to the cafeteria for tater tots and fish sticks.

Marcus served as emcee and would close the show, which he acknowledged was unconventional, but he explained such an arrangement was necessary in light of his abilities both as a magician and as a showman. No one felt compelled to argue with him.

At exactly 12:01 p.m., Marcus gave the nod to Ms. Gold, who volunteered to run the music system. Two things in that description are somewhat misleading. Ms. Gold volunteered in the sense that Principal Haynes told her she had a choice of monitoring the event or cancelling it. Ms. Gold thought a missed lunch was probably less irksome than listening to Marcus complain bitterly for the remainder of the school year, so, there she was. No one was willing to actually run tech from the booth, so Ms. Gold ran a "sound system" that consisted of Marcus' portable tape deck with the volume cranked up to the point of distortion. On Marcus's cue, Ms. Gold sighed and pushed play, which caused the speakers to emit some horrid combination of Gregorian chants and electronic music.

From backstage, Marcus began to speak into the one microphone available for the show.

"Since the dawn of time," Marcus intoned, "man has sought to harness the magic in our world and bend it to his will. Today we shall do that very thing. For today, you shall see magic under the control of the Mystic Order of Broncos right here in the Hall of Miracles. Prepare yourself and be...amazed!"

Marcus walked out on stage, carrying the microphone and stand with him. He was dressed in a tuxedo with a long, black cape. He set the stand down and spread his arms to take in the applause of the crowd. One guy clapped. Another merely said, "Nice cape." No exclamation point.

After an uncomfortable moment, Marcus gestured at Ms. Gold to turn off the music, which she did, failing to fade it as he had shown her before. It just came to an abrupt stop. Someone coughed.

"Ladies and gentlemen, we, the Mystic Order of Broncos, invite you to accompany us on a journey into the world of magic and wonder! I am your host, Marco Mysterio, and I bid you welcome!" Marcus held for applause that was not forthcoming.

"Thank you!" he said, apparently oblivious to the complete lack of enthusiasm. "Without further ado, please welcome the Astonishing Ally!

Ally's act consisted of a brief speech about the history of juggling, after which she juggled pins and balls and scarves with reasonable skill. She only dropped twice. Ally was followed by Nick doing two card tricks. Whether the tricks were well executed was lost on the audience, who could not see the cards from their seats. However, the audience volunteer (and it took nearly five minutes to secure one), reported that Nick had not, in fact, selected his card. Stan made a plush toy rabbit levitate, almost convincingly, apart from the plainly visible string attached from the rabbit to his magic wand. Marcus was going to close the show with an illusion involving an apparent escape from a burlap bag. But, "the day's penultimate act of magic most astonishing" was Jim, or as he was called for stage purpose, "Jimmy Gandalf," a name which was Marcus' idea. It was not a good name, but everyone admitted it was better than "The Great TopDini".

Jim walked onto stage carrying a black plastic briefcase that his father had given him when he needed something to carry his various Dungeons & Dragons rulebooks. The case was covered in stickers with such witty statements as "Warning! Contents Protected by Magic!" Jim was just wearing his regular school clothes, jeans with a bunched up, barely tucked in button-down blue shirt.

Jim set the case down and approached the mic, at which point he was struck by a jolt of nearly crippling stage fright as well as some nasty feedback from the microphone.

"Um, watch this red silk," he said after an excruciating twenty seconds of silence.

Jim took the cheap red silk in his right hand, and stuffed it into his left, in which he was palming a false thumb. He stuffed the silk into the fake thumb in an effort to make it disappear. His hands were slick with sweat, and he dropped the metal thumb. It clanked to the stage with the end of the silk protruding from it like a scarlet tail.

The audience laughed as Jim picked up the thumb, shoving it into his pocket.

Jim reached into his plastic briefcase and pulled out two silvery metal rings. He held them up and said, "Um, two solid metal rings, see?"

He clinked the rings together to prove they were metal, and, indeed solid. "I'm going to make them, um, connect by magic," he said, sweat beading on his forehead.

Jim rubbed the rings together while saying random words in Latin ("Puella est Agricola!"). He managed to pull off the trick, whereby one ring goes through the cut-out portion of the other. He held the now "magically" joined rings up for the audience to see. He got a small amount of, mainly ironic, applause. Energized by this modicum of approval, Jim started to take a bow. In doing so, he whipped his hands down, causing one of the rings to sling the other into the air. The loose ring caromed across the wooden floor and spun for an impressively long time before collapsing to the stage.

The audience laughed at Jim. "Nice one, Gandalf!" someone shouted. Jim grabbed the ring off the floor and threw it into his briefcase. He grabbed the case, forgetting to latch it, and turned to flee the stage. The case fell open and various gewgaws, doodads, and thingamajigs poured out onto the stage. Jim collapsed to the ground and scooped up his magical props, shoving them back in the case. Holding the case to his chest, he stumbled off stage.

The audience hooted and hurled insults at the stage. Ms. Gold looked at her watch and declared that the show was over, even though there were ten minutes left in the period.

Marcus was tempted to argue, but even he realized that his amazing illusion work would be no match for the contempt of the crowds.

"Ladies and gentlemen," Marcus said, "this concludes the Mystic Order of Broncos premiere performance of astonishment! We thank you for feasting on our talents! Until next time . . . believe!"

He left the stage with a flourish and no applause.

Reviews for the program ranged from the generic "That sucked!" to the more personalized "You suck!"

The Mystic Order of Broncos met the next day at the Sorcerers' Table. Despite Marcus' efforts to raise morale, the magicians were inconsolable. The Broncos were broken.

The group continued to meet for lunch, but that was more a function of avoiding derision than it was to discuss the craft of magic.

There would not be a second performance by the Order, and Jim threw his black plastic case on a shelf in his closet where it would remain untouched and protected by magic for years.

***

Jim did not try to do magic again for many years. He and the rest of the Mystic Order of Broncos decided it was time to just get through high school without suffering an emotional or physical beating at the hands of the kids that were cooler than them, which was most the class. The only exception was Marcus. He kept at it, managing to do a birthday party here, a state fair there, and he even appeared on *Mel Hall's Magic Menagerie*. Granted it was Sunday morning at 8, and Marcus only did a four-minute spot, but television is television, and by Andy Warhol's reckoning he still had eleven minutes of fame left in him.

After high school, Jim went to a state college about an hour and a half from home. He studied accounting, and his college career was only moderately better than his high school days. He shed some of his youthful huskiness and got a girlfriend – his first – during the fall of his sophomore year. By spring she had moved on to greener pastures. Literally, she had to move back home to her family farm in Mississippi due to her father's health issues. While there, she reunited with her high school boyfriend. They were married within a year.

Jim graduated with a degree in accounting. After two years in the rough and tumble accountancy trenches in a small company, Jim decided he needed a stronger act. The next year he returned to Memphis, and enrolled in the MBA program at the local university. He also moved back in with his parents, who had kept his room exactly as he had left it, magic briefcase and all.

The summer before grad school started, Jim was watching late night TV, as he was want to do in lieu of getting out of the house. Nestled between an interview with Kevin Pollak and a woman who played musical spoons (with startling proficiency), was a magician introduced as Marco Blade.

Marco Blade was Marcus Wade. Marcus performed two elaborate, well-executed illusions, and spent a few minutes talking to the show's host, who mainly made wisecracks about magicians and, for some reason, ham.

As Jim watched the show, he went on an emotional journey. First there was surprise, which drifted into happiness, before veering into depression and jealousy. The odyssey concluded with a melancholic longing to reconnect with lost friends and magic. And then he ate a sandwich.

Two weeks after graduate school started, Jim picked up a copy of the campus' student newspaper, *The Daily Growl*, which was a terrible name because the publication only came out three days a week, and growled on none of them. He flipped through stories of campus crime (there had been a fight at a fraternity house, allegedly over a hat, and someone stole a basket of wet laundry from one of the dorms – it was unclear if any hats were in the basket) before he saw the ad for events that week at the student union.

Emblazoned beneath a photo of Marcus with his arms spread out as he appeared to fly were the words "As Seen On National TV, Catch MARCO BLADE, Master Illusionist! Tickets Free With Student ID!"

Jim had two thoughts. One was that he would go to the show. The other was that Stan Huang would be pissed that Marcus was doing levitation now.

***

For a magic show at a local university, Marco Blade's performance was reasonably well attended. Jim walked in by himself about twenty minutes before the show, and took a seat in the nearly empty ninth row. As he sat down, he heard someone call his name.

"Jim, is that you?"

He turned and saw Ally Barnes walking up to him.

"Oh, hey, Ally!" Jim said, happy to see his old magician-in-arms. "I didn't know you were in town." The two awkwardly avoided a hug.

"I came back after graduation," Ally said. "I've got a job with Battle & Mann."

Battle & Mann was an intermodal shipping company based in Memphis. It was one of the city's top 20 employers, and handled barge, rail, and truck transportation of all sorts of freight. Mainly rocks. Ally had studied industrial engineering in Illinois, and she was employed with the company in a junior analyst role while she worked on her master's degree.

Jim asked Ally to sit with him as he filled her in on his plans before they caught up on the members of the Mystic Order of the Broncos.

They were both excited to see that Marcus was doing well, and agreed his television appearance was good. As far as they knew, Marcus was the only Bronco still practicing the magical arts.

Ally had heard from Stan, who had gone to college in Arizona, where he interned senior year with a manufacturing facility. He started a job after graduation as a front-line supervisor, but was assured he would be in middle management within a year. Two tops.

Nick had gone to a small liberal arts school in Arkansas and graduated with a degree in political science, before enrolling in Ole Miss law school in Oxford, Mississippi. He was heading into his third and final year. Both Ally and Jim had gotten save the date cards for Nick's wedding to his long-time girlfriend, Erin, set for March 15 the following year. Erin's family was from Oxford, so the wedding would take place there.

After catching up, Jim and Ally reminisced about the ill-fated lunch show and discussed how much, or, more appropriately, how little, they had both kept up with performing.

"I still juggle sometimes," Ally said. "It doesn't come up much. Because, it's juggling. But I'm going to try to get back into the Ren Faire thing now that I'm back home." Ally was a member of Medieval Realms, a group that gathered once a month in the park. Many members wore homemade armor, and wailed on each other with foam covered sticks that they pretended were swords. Ally was not one of the stick-bangers. She would show up at the annual Renaissance Faire and juggle as part of a street performance show. Occasionally she would man the "mead" stand, which was just warm store-bought cider. But you would sometimes get a "huzzah" when you bought one to make it an authentic medieval treat.

The lights in the auditorium dimmed, and a loud mixture of techno and something vaguely Middle Eastern filled the room. A booming voice overwhelmed the music.

"Throughout time, there have been those whose feats have mystified and amazed all who beheld them. Beggars and kings alike have stood in awe of these rare and powerful individuals, and now you will join the company of those privileged few who have borne witness to feats that can change the lives of those who behold them. Please take your place in history and welcome the incomparable Marco Blade!"

The music swelled as the audience applauded appropriately for the venue, but not nearly to a level high enough to match the bombastic introduction. Ally and Jim looked at each other and laughed.

There was a loud explosion and a column of smoke illuminated by green light billowed up from the stage. As the smoke cleared, Marco Blade emerged, wearing black pants, a white shirt unbuttoned by one too many buttons, and a black cape with red lining.

The audience, already unclear as to how much they were supposed to applaud for the intro music, gave Marco a round of applause that was clearly not up to his standards, having now appeared on a segment of a late-night television show.

"You believe you have come to witness parlor tricks," Marco said removing his cape with a flourish. "But what your brain expects to see is not always what your eyes allow it to see."

He swished the cape around and re-opened it to reveal to the audience that the lining was now green. Jim and Ally looked at each other and nodded. The trick was well executed. The audience was mildly impressed.

Marco Blade proceeded to fill the next hour and a half with a series of well-executed illusions, and witty, albeit stilted, banter. He involved reluctant audience members in his act, and even made a table and then himself seem to rise off the stage into the air by a few feet.

Jim and Ally would later agree that the show was better than they expected and that Marcus had gotten quite good at his craft.

After the show, Jim and Ally managed to get backstage and found Marcus' dressing room, which was a bathroom with a piece of paper Scotch taped to the door on which someone had used a large black felt tip pen to write "Mark Blade". One of the campus security guys tried to stop them from entering, but when Ally said, "We are friends of his," the guard seemed unable to argue with this evidence, and let them in.

Marcus stood up from the folding metal chair he was sitting on to take off his stage makeup when he saw them. "Do my eyes deceive me! I cannot believe that the incomparable Ally Barnes and the amazing Jim Lane stand before me! Friends, how are you? It has, indeed, been too long!"

They chatted amicably for a few minutes when there was a knock at the door. "Marco, we got to clear out," the person knocking said from the other said.

"Ah, my friends, I regret I must take leave of you and the facility. We have another show in another town. Show business is a cruel spouse, indeed. Speaking of, are you going to Nick's wedding?"

"I plan to," Ally said.

"Yeah, me too," Jim said.

"Excellent! Then, if I do not see you before, I will definitely see you come Ides of March! Beware!"

"Sounds good," Ally said.

"Until then, my friends, it has been a joy and a privilege. Stay magical," Marcus said as he opened the door for them.

As they left, a tall, older man, dressed in a white linen suit and sporting a well-manicured cotton white mustache and goatee walked past. He raised a black walking stick to his forehead in salute before walking into Marcus' dressing room without a knock.

"If I didn't know any better, I'd swear that was Colonel Sanders," Jim said.

"Just thinner," Ally said.

***

Jim and Ally went to a coffee shop near campus after they left Marcus' show.

"Stay magical?" Jim asked, swirling his coffee mug. "Did he really say that?"

"He did." Ally said, smiling thinly. She brushed a strand of her chestnut hair off her face. "I would have assumed he'd have stopped talking like that by now. But, it's just gotten worse."

Jim laughed. "I guess it works for him."

"Fame takes a person's dumb qualities and makes them dumber," Ally said.

"That's profound," Jim said.

"I'm a very profound and serious person, Jim."

Jim looked at her and nodded, and there was an awkward silence that seemed to last a month.

"Anyway," Ally said, breaking the stalemate, "you're going to the wedding?"

"Sure," Jim said.

"I'm surprised you aren't in the wedding party."

"He's got three brothers, and he was in a Mississippi fraternity. I never had a chance."

"Weird. I'm in it," Ally said.

"You are?"

"No, idiot."

Jim nodded, and took the final sip from his cup, "Well, I guess I'll see you there, yeah?"

"You know we both live here now, right?" Ally said, putting down her cup.

"Yeah."

"So, if we want to see each other, we don't have to wait until to March."

"True," Jim said, unable to follow up with anything cogent.

"Hey, dummy," Ally said. "Ask me out to dinner Friday."

"Oh, sure. Yeah. Do you want to go to dinner Friday?"

"Sorry, I'm busy," Ally said.

"Ah, ok." Jim said.

"I'll see you Friday," Ally said with a laugh. "Want to pick me up, or I can meet you if you're worried it'll be a nightmare."

Jim decided to pick her up. And that's how two members of the Mystic Order of Broncos went from being solo acts to being a two-person show.

***

Nick and Erin's wedding and reception were held at Bellington House, a large, white antebellum mansion outside of Oxford. It had, in very different times, been the family home on a plantation, but now served as a venue for weddings, parties, and the occasional frat party.

Nick had grown up Baptist, while Erin was a Methodist. Because Nick had never been particularly devout, and because everyone agreed alcohol was an important part of the festivities, the Methodist side won that particular holy war.

Jim and Ally had cleaned up nicely for the wedding. He wore a blue suit with a white shirt that was only slightly rumpled and a red tie, and she had on a light green dress. They almost looked like grownups, even if Jim's white shirt tenaciously fought to untuck itself throughout the proceedings. They entered the ballroom, and glanced around. Neither of them knew many of Nick's friends, and didn't know any of Erin's family or members of her social circle. A young woman stood at the front of the room playing a violin. A teenage boy sat behind her holding a trumpet in one hand and carrying a bored expression on his acne-scarred face. On the other side of the room at the front, an older woman sat behind a piano, flipping through sheet music, and occasionally smiling or waving at people as they entered the ballroom.

"Where do you want to sit?" Jim asked.

"On the groom's side," Ally said.

"Yeah, ok," Jim said, without moving.

"That's the right side, babe," Ally said.

"Oh, yeah," Jim said, pausing again.

"Our right. Not stage right," Ally said, nudging Jim with her shoulder.

Shortly after sitting down in an otherwise empty row, someone behind them said, "Hey, is that the magician's row!"

The turned and saw Stan Huang standing behind them with a big grin on his face.

Ally shot up and hugged him as Jim got to his feet.

"I didn't expect to see you here, Stan!" Ally said. "Gosh, what's it been, four years?"

"That might be right," Stan said. "Christmas Freshman year, maybe? Jim, how have you been?"

"Good," Jim said. "I've started my MBA. What about you?"

"I just got my black belt," Stan said.

"Oh, congrats. I didn't know you were doing martial arts."

"It's a process certification, you racist," Stan said with a deadpan face. "You just assume I'm a karate guy?"

"I, no, I'm sorry," Jim said, looking at Ally, who shrugged.

"I'm messing with you. But it really is a big deal for me. And I did karate as a kid. Only made it to green belt."

"Well come sit with us, you Six Sigma jackass," Ally said to Stan, who laughed and sat next to them.

"Last time I saw you, you were dating some guy named Bearclaw or something like that," Stan said to Ally. "Is that still going on?"

"Not exactly," Ally said.

"He seemed weird," Stan said.

"He was normal for the Ren Faire crowd. Besides, he could recite the Canterbury Tales in the original Middle English, so what girl could resist?"

Ally looked at Jim. "My current beau is a huge improvement in every possible way."

"Why didn't you bring him?" Stan asked.

"I did."

Jim looked up and comprehension dawned on Stan's face.

"Are you serious?" he asked, and after a beat said "Way to go Jim! You probably better learn some Chaucer, though."

"Wouldn't hurt," Ally said. "Learn some of the bawdy stuff. It's surprisingly effective."

"Holy crap, we have a celebrity sighting," Stan said, pointing towards the ballroom's double doors. Marcus, wearing an immaculate tuxedo, was making his entrance.

"Marco Blade!" Stan bellowed at Marcus, who had just spotted the group. Marcus smiled as he approached.

"Stan Huang!" Marcus said, joining the group. "You look fantastic, my friend. Do you still have your hands in magic?"

"I mean, I can make stuff appear just in time, so that's pretty magical."

Marcus nodded as if he had any idea what Stan was talking about. His magical knowledge did not extend to the intricacies of industrial engineering and supply chain logistics.

"Hey Marcus," Jim said.

"Jim and Ally, good to see you again! Anything new and exciting with you?

"They're dating," said Stan.

"How long has that been the case?" Marcus said, raising his left eyebrow.

"You're show was our first date," Ally said.

"Wait, that counts?" Jim asked.

"Sure. It makes a better story than 'awkward coffee date,'" Ally said.

"I am glad my mystical powers helped bring you two together," Marcus laughed, clapping Jim and Ally's shoulders. "I make no claims of having the ability to cast a charme d'amour, but the credit I shall take nonetheless!"

"So, nice place for a wedding," Ally said, trying to change the subject because Jim was clearly not too interested in discussing the d'amour issue with Marcus or Stan.

"It's like *Gone with the Wind* in here," Stan said.

"Not entirely, thank goodness," Marcus said.

"Oh yeah, right," Stan said. "Sorry, Marcus."

Before the group had a chance to unpack the relevant social issues they were facing, the violinist stopped. The older lady began to play the piano. The trumpeter still looked bored.

"I think that's our cue to sit down," Ally said.

The processional began a minute or two later. The wedding ceremony was lovely. Erin was radiant. Nick was clearly nervous. The priest made a couple of jokes that got the appropriate level of laughter. And, ultimately, the teenage trumpet player (who turned out to be Erin's younger brother) got to play for the recessional. Despite his ennui, the kid was pretty good.

***

The reception connected the expected dots. Some dancing. Some eating. And drinking. Too much of the latter than was reasonable.

Nick was happy to see his old magic friends. They talked at the reception for a little while, though the groom's attention was split among multiple well-wishers, and relatives both old and new.

Following the reception, the Mystic Order of the Broncos (sans Nick) walked – or staggered as the case may be – across the street to the hotel where they were all staying. Marcus did not drink having noted that "A true magician's mind must never be muddled!" He remained immaculately dressed. The rest of them looked a little worse for wear.

Ally and Stan had grabbed a couple of unused bottles of wine each, and Ally insisted they all continue the party in Jim's and her room. "It's like a suite. It's a sweet suite. There's, like, this whole separate room with chairs and a couch. It's fancy as hell," she explained.

Ally and Jim took the couch. Jim had his shirt untucked, with his undone red tie dangling from his collar. Ally kicked off her shoes and threw her legs across Jim's lap. Stan slouched into a vaguely comfortable blue upholstered chair, his jacket thrown on the floor. Marcus sat straight up in the other blue chair. He had loosened his tie slightly, but that was the only concession he made to lower his sartorial standards for the evening's revels. He did not unbutton his top shirt button. Three of the wine bottles were empty before anyone seemed to notice.

"If I ever needed a lawyer in Mississippi, I'd hire Nick," Jim said. "I bet he's going to be great at it."

"He's got charisma, I'll give him that," Ally said. "Probably doesn't hurt."

"Charisma can carry one far, indeed," Marcus said.

"Under what set of circumstances would you ever need a lawyer in Mississippi?" Stan asked.

"I don't know. Speeding or stealing a cow or something," Jim said with a slur.

"Hopefully both charges aren't part of the same crime spree," Ally said. "Would one of you open up that last bottle, please?"

"Why don't you do it," Stan asked.

"I don't want to; it's way over there by you," Ally said while vaguely pointing.

"That's, like three feet," said Stan.

"The math is in my favor!" Ally proclaimed.

Stan begrudgingly shifted in his chair and grabbed the bottle on the small, wooden coffee table. They had finagled a corkscrew from the front desk earlier, and Stan twisted out the cork, dropping it on the table before pouring Ally, Jim, and himself glasses of merlot. He then collapsed into his chair.

"Thank you, black belt," Ally said, taking a sip from her glass. "Hand me the cork."

"No. Why?" Stan said.

"It's got a design thingy on it that I want to look at."

"Nope. I got up already. I probably can't pull that off again for an hour," Stan said, closing his eyes.

"Babe, hand me the cork," Ally said to Jim.

Jim reached toward the table half-heartedly. "It's too far. Sorry."

"Please," Ally said, laughing.

"Fine," Jim said, waving his hand dismissively.

The cork moved, rolling a couple of inches towards Ally.

Ally smirked, assuming she had just witnessed an amusing coincidence. "Nice! Do that again!"

Jim laughed absently and waved his hand.

The cork rolled another inch.

Ally and Jim both laughed. Marcus leaned forward.

"Jim, see if you can move it the other way," Marcus said.

"Like this," Jim said, waving his hand in the opposite direction than he had previously, and the cork rolled away from Ally.

Jim and Ally stopped laughing. They both hazily looked at each other as Marcus stood up.

"Let me see your hands, Jim," Marcus demanded.

Jim held up his hands as Marcus closely inspected and prodded them. He picked up the cork and inspected it, before looking around the room, paying close attention to the rectangular air conditioning unit on the floor by the room's window facing the parking lot.

"Do it again," Marcus said in a serious tone.

Jim shrugged and waved his hand back and forth. The cork rolled in apparent compliance with Jim's commands. Ally threw her legs to the ground and leaned forward looking at the cork.

"Jim, wave up this time," Marcus said.

Jim raised his hand and left it pointing upwards. The cork trembled on the table before rising barely off the surface. It shook, floating for less than a second before falling.

"What just happened?" Ally asked.

"I'll tell you what just happened," Marcus said. "Jimmy Gandalf just performed the only real magic anyone has ever seen."

At that moment, Stan snored.

***

It was shortly before three in the morning before Marcus left, helping Stan make his way to his room. A farewell brunch was scheduled for the now seemingly ungodly hour of 10:00 on Sunday morning.

Ally woke up slightly before 9:00 and nudged Jim awake, despite his remarkable resistance to her efforts. They both cleaned up and got dressed with enormous effort, managing only to incoherently grunt at each other as they battled the haze brought on by sleep deprivation and wine.

After Jim finished dressing, he asked Ally, "Does this look ok?"

"Yeah," Ally said. "So, are we going to talk about last night?"

"If you want to."

"If I want to? Of course, I want to. You think we are just going to ignore the fact that you have suddenly become a sorcerer."

"No I didn't. It's not like I summoned a demon," he said.

"So, you aren't going to deny you actually did magic?"

"I guess not."

Ally kissed Jim, and laughed. "That's as close to bragging as I've ever heard from you. You're sure, though, right?"

Jim turned to the bathroom counter and waved his hand at the plastic cup by the sink. It wobbled.

"I'm sure."

"Ho-lee crap," Ally said in a low, almost reverential voice. She paused, and then, switching to manic delight, said "Make it fly over here!"

Jim said, "I can't."

"Try!"

Jim waved at the cup, and it failed to take flight. It barely rattled on the counter.

"That's it. That's all I can do," Jim said lowering his hand. "Sorry."

"Don't apologize because you aren't whooshing stuff around the room," Ally said, looking him in the eyes. "You can do something no one, and I mean no one, else on the planet can do. It's miraculous!"

There was a knock on the hotel room door, and Ally walked towards it. "Miraculous," she said.

She opened the door, and Marcus was standing outside, dressed remarkably casually for him. He had on a sports coat but no tie. It was a weekend full of miracles.

"Ally, Jim, how are you both this morning?" Marcus asked with the usual theatricality in his voice dialed down. "Can I come in?"

Ally invited him in and closed the door.

"Jim, we all know that you performed actual magic last night. That's why I wanted to catch you before brunch," Marcus said. "I need you to promise me you will not do it again in front of other people. Not right now."

"Jealous, Marcus? Ally asked with a chuckle.

"I am," Marcus said. "But that's not why am I asking this. I wanted to stop you before brunch so you didn't show off your new skills...or, I guess, powers."

"Why?" Jim asked.

"You need to let the right people see this first, so you can make sure you don't squander this."

"Squander it? How would I do that?"

"Jim, Ally's not wrong. I am beyond jealous. But, I am also your friend, and I know this is a once in a lifetime, maybe a once in a forever, situation. I just want to make sure that you meet with people who can help you make the most of it. This is huge, Jim. You need to follow a path to success with this gift."

Jim nodded. "What should I do, Marcus?"

"My next gig is in St. Louis in a couple of weeks. I'll be home until then. Why don't I come to your home tomorrow after you get off work and we see what we see?"

"If that's okay with Ally, sure," Jim said.

"Living in sin, are we!" Marcus said, the usual theatricality creeping back into his voice.

"Nothing but sin, all the time," Ally said. "Yes, please come to the apartment at about 6:30. I'll email you the address. We can have dinner then we can talk about whatever the hell this is."

"A plan is formed!" Marcus said, clapping his hands together once. "I will see you tomorrow evening. Until then, let no one see what you can do!"

There was a knock at the door, and Ally opened it. Stan was standing there, his acute hangover apparent. "Hey guys, you going to brunch. Sorry I crashed last night. Did I miss anything?"

"Nothing other than a few miracles," Ally said.

"Huh?" Stan asked.

"Come on, let's get some mimosas," Ally said.

***

Dinner the next night was nothing fancy. Jim and Ally ordered pizza, and Marcus brought over a bottle of wine that they all agreed paired well with pepperoni.

"Alright, Jim," Marcus said. "Have you got a grasp on what you can and cannot do?"

"It's only small things," Jim said. "It feels like I am – I don't know – projecting a hand, if that makes sense. I have to be able to grab the object easily. So, I can move a cork, like you saw. But I can't pick up a piece of paper, because I just can't get the mental fingers around it. And, it can't be too big either. Even if it doesn't weigh a lot, it seems like I can only affect stuff that is small. I know this sounds ridiculous."

"How much weight can you lift?" Marcus said, ignoring Jim's downplaying of his ability.

"I don't know. Not much."

Marcus stood up and retrieved a backpack he had brought with them. He opened it and pulled out a rectangular black velvet box. He opened it, revealing a red velvet interior that nestled ten small rounded brass objects.

"What are those?" Ally asked.

"Weights, ranging from one to ten grams," Marcus said, nonchalantly.

"You carry around a box full of little weights?" Ally asked.

"Not all the time, but I use them to help design illusions," Marcus said.

"Like you do," Ally said.

Marcus smiled and took the smallest weight out of the box and placed it on the coffee table. "Can you move that, Jim?"

Jim waved his hand and the small weight moved half an inch in the direction of his hand movement.

"Can you lift it?" Marcus asked.

Jim motioned and the weight rose slightly, but visibly off the table before falling a split second later."

"Well, we know you can handle one gram," Marcus said. "Let's jump ahead, shall we!"

Marcus replaced the one gram brass weight with an eight gram. After repeated efforts, Jim could not move it at all. After further experiments, they determined that Jim could almost imperceptibly move a five-gram weight. The heaviest weight he could lift, even momentarily, was four grams. Further experimentation showed that Jim could not move any amount of weight if there was any significant resistance. He couldn't unzip a zipper or unbutton a button, both of which Ally suggested pointing out that's what James Bond would try if he could do magic.

After a couple of hours, Jim said he was tired. "I don't know if it's because it's late or because...this...wears me out."

"The wine may not be helping either," Ally said.

"Let's not push this," Marcus said. "Keep working on it. Are you free Thursday night?"

Jim looked at Ally, and she said "We are. Do you want to come over? I'll actually cook something."

Marcus held up a hand. "No, kind though the offer is. I think I need to take Jim to meet some...people. I need to clear an invitation for you both, but under the circumstances, I do not see how it is possible one would not be forthcoming."

"Who do you want us to see?" Jim asked.

"I want you to meet the Southern Magi. It will change your life. And perhaps the world of magic itself."

**

Hidden in an alleyway near a rib joint in downtown Memphis is the home of the Southern Magi. The edifice is a nondescript stone building with two doors set about ten feet apart. Most people, if they gave any thought to it at all, would assume the building was an abandoned store front, or the office of a solo personal injury lawyer.

Marcus met Jim and Ally in a surface parking lot about a block from the building, and led them to the location. When they reached the building, Marcus removed a chain necklace with a key attached from around his neck. He looked around to make sure he was not being observed, and then unlocked the door on the right, holding it open for his guests.

"Enter freely, and prepare for wonders heretofore unknown," he said.

"Something more amazing that actual magic?" Ally asked with a hint of sarcasm.

"Right, just go in."

Behind the door was a poorly lit old, brown wooden stairway leading down below street level. They walked single file down the stairs, each footstep filling the air with ominous creeks and groans.

"Are you going to kill us, Marcus?" Jim asked with a nervous laugh.

"We shall see what the night brings," Marcus said in a deeper than usual voice.

"Well, that's on you," Ally said to Jim.

They reached the bottom of the staircase, which ended in front of a faded white wooden door. Marcus pushed forward and knocked twice rapidly, waiting a moment before rapping once again on the door, followed by another brief pause and three quick knocks.

The door opened, and a tall, wiry man in a tuxedo greeted them.

"Speak the name and enter," the man said in a strong Southern accent that did not fit the tuxedo or solemnity of the greeting.

"Djedi's loaves," Marcus said gravely.

The man smiled stepping aside, "Come on in Marcus, how you been, man?"

"Good, Derrick," Marcus said. "Doing my part to keep the world magical!"

"I heard that," Derrick said. "They told me you were bringing guests. Y'all come on in!"

The group walked past Derrick and into a room that had no business being in the building they had entered. An almost golden light permeated the room that appeared to be a lounge. Framed portraits hung on the walls along with colorful vintage posters featuring magicians summoning spirits and conferring with Satan or skeletons.

Around ten men and a few women, along with a couple of high school students, stood or sat in the red velvet upholstered couches and wingback chairs were scattered throughout the space. One very old man sat in a wheelchair and watched Jim. A woman stood at the built-in bar in a lighted niche in one corner of the room chatting with the bartender. A closed red velvet curtain ran the length of one wall.

"Marcus, here you are!" said a man standing to greet them. He wore a white linen suit and had a nearly matching goatee and mustache. He limped towards them, relying on a black walking stick.

Jim and Ally looked at each other with a smile.

"Magister!" Marcus said bowing slightly, "Please allow me to introduce my friends Ally Barnes and Jim Lane. Jim and Ally, this is Magister Wyatt Taylor."

"Mr. Lane, I have heard much about you, sir," Wyatt said. "I must confess, I find what I hear to be rather incredible at best."

"Yeah. It's pretty weird, sir," Jim said.

"If anyone other than my esteemed mentee had told me the things I have heard, I'd have ignored the fool or given him a good whack, depending on my disposition at the moment."

Wyatt narrowed his eyes. "We shall see if you are spared that fate, Mr. Lane," he said shaking his stick. "Ms. Barnes, it is a pleasure."

Wyatt limped away.

"Do all of you talk like that," Ally asked Marcus.

"Like what?" Marcus asked.

A teenage girl in all black with deep purple hair walked up to the group. "So, you're the wizard," she said looking at Jim. Her voice was flat, without a trace of sarcasm or humor.

"What, no," said Jim. "I'm just a..."

"A wizard," the girl said with a serious expression on her face. Her mouth, adorned with a small lip ring, did not show a hint of a smile.

"I'm Jim," he said, holding out his hand.

The girl looked at him, her purple lidded eyes seeming to appraise him. "Yes," she said, and walked off.

"What's with Wynona Ryder?" Ally asked.

"That's Dara Starr," Marcus said. "She's an up and coming practitioner. She's our youngest active, a high school junior. She's really quite good, just a little odd at times."

"Honored members and guests," Derrick said loudly from beside the curtain. "It is time to convene. Members cloak yourselves in magic and enter the Sanctum!"

Derrick drew back the curtain to reveal a small auditorium.

Marcus nodded and Ally and Jim, and walked towards the curtain.

"Come on, Wizard, let's see how this goes," Ally said.

Inside the auditorium, wooden folding chairs faced a small stage illuminated by overhead lighting. Like the entry room, there were no windows. The wooden floor was laid out with diagonal patterns. On either side of the space just past the curtain, built-in racks lined the walls. Hanging from these racks were black capes with red lining.

Marcus took a cape from the rack and put it on. Above some of the capes on the racks were black velvet bags. Marcus took the one above where his cape had been and pulled out a magician's wand that had been painted gold.

"What is that?" Jim asked.

"My golden wand. A high honor not lightly given, my friend," Marcus said.

Jim looked around at the other members donning their capes. Some had wands, but most did not.

"Are we supposed to put on capes?" Jim asked.

"Only members have that privilege...and grave responsibility," Marcus said.

"I think you are overstating that a bit," Ally said. "I mean, it's just a cape."

"I can understand how you may feel that way. But, you shall just have to trust me, it is much more," Marcus said.

Jim nodded. He was a little disappointed that he didn't get to wear a cape.

Marcus ushered them to their chairs and Magister Taylor walked up to the stage, which had a lectern and a folding card table covered with a black cloth. The combination of Wyatt's white suit and black cape was striking. The golden wand in one hand and the black walking stick in the other added to the picture. Taylor set the wand on the lectern and addressed the audience. As he spoke, it was clear that he could captivate an audience with an almost palpable air of authority.

"Good evening," Wyatt said. "We will forego our normal course of announcements and business this evening. We will dispense with the usual greetings and glad-handing, because we have in our midst one who claims to possess magic. Not tricks. Not illusions. Actual magic."

Jim looked nervously at Marcus, who nodded slightly.

"The claim is a bold one," Wyatt continued. "Oh, it's been heard before. Usually, though, it is a declaration made to audiences, not to fellow followers of the art. Some would say such a claim is either mere braggadocio or evidence of a delusional mind. But tonight, one of our own – a holder of a golden wand, no less – has vouched for these claims. He says he has witnessed them himself, and warrants that there is no artifice at play. Brother Marcus, have I spoken accurately?"

Marcus rose to his feet. "You have, Magister. I have witnessed this firsthand and hereby swear by the wand that this man possesses the ability to perform feats of actual magic," he said gesturing at Jim with a dramatic sweep of his arm.

Wyatt nodded. "Mr. Lane, do you stand by these claims?"

Jim was caught off guard. He looked up at Marcus and to Ally. They both nodded. "Yeah," Jim said.

"Would you be so kind as to rise and speak up, sir," Wyatt said.

Jim got to his feet, and said, "Yes. I do."

"Very good, sir. We are all either in for the spectacle of a lifetime, or a moment of laughter. Either is welcome, though truly the former is why we are all here. Mr. Lane, please join me."

Jim walked hesitantly towards the stage. As he did, the eyes of the room bored into him. His footsteps echoed throughout the auditorium. When Jim reached the stage, Taylor spread out his arms and said, "Esteemed Southern Magi, please give a warm welcome to the man who proclaims he alone possesses magic . . . true magic. Please welcome Jim Lane!"

The audience applauded politely.

"Thank you, sir," Jim said. "What do you want me to do?"

"Your act, son. Do your act." Wyatt said with a kindly smile.

"I . . . can't," Jim said.

"And why might that be?"

"I don't have one," Jim said.

Nervous laughter trickled throughout the audience.

"Well, that does present quite the conundrum," Wyatt said. "Brother Marcus, can you help this poor, actless fellow out?"

Marcus strode to the stage, and was greeted by markedly more enthusiastic applause.

"You are, as always, too kind," Marcus said with a small bow.

He put his arm around Jim and whispered into his ear, "Just do your thing, Jim."

"With what?"

"Does anyone have a pen or pencil we could borrow?" Marcus asked the audience.

"I do," said Dana, the teenager who had talked to Jim earlier. She walked up to the stage, pulling a plastic Bic pen from the backpack she carried with her.

"Thank you," Marcus said. "Please give the pen to Magister Taylor for inspection."

Wyatt accepted the pen and looked at it. "It is, by all appearance a perfectly normal pen," he said approvingly.

"Excellent," said Marcus. He walked to the card table and whipped the black cloth off it and onto the ground in a dramatic flourish.

"Magister, please place the pen on the table. Do not let either Jim or I touch it. And, if you do not mind, please confirm that there is nothing under the table."

Wyatt placed the pen on the table and looked under the table before stepping back. "There is nothing under that table," he said pointing at it. "And nothing on top of it except for Sister Starr's pen."

Marcus nodded. "Fellow Magi, you are now about to witness a miracle. Mark this day well."

Marcus looked at his friend and said, "Jim, show them the magic!"

Jim stepped forward and looked at the audience.

"Okay, hi," Jim said. "I am going to move that pen."

Jim raised his hand and swept it left. The pen slowly rolled along the surface of the table. He moved it the other direction and the pen followed.

"Thank you" Jim said.

Several of the audience members muttered in confusion. "That's it?" one person said a little too loudly. Wyatt walked over to Jim.

"Son, show me your hands."

Jim allowed the Magister to examine his hands. He picked up the pen again and looked it over. "I find no strings. No magnets. No indicia of any artifice," Wyatt said. "There is no natural explanation for what we have just seen.

"Remote control! Someone's working a remote control," Jerry Randolph, a heavyset middle-aged man in the audience shouted.

"It's not," Jim said.

"Ha!" Jerry said. "It's not even a good bit of showmanship. You wasted our time for this?"

"It's not a remote control," Jim said, a trace of unexpected anger sneaking into his voice.

"Boring!" Jerry said, and murmurs from the audience indicated the Magi were siding with him.

"You think this is a ridiculous remote control? You think this is, what, a store bough trick?" Marcus thundered. "You want to test him, then bring yourself up here now."

"Gladly!" Jerry said as he trundled towards the stage.

"And just so the rest of you don't think Brother Randolph is in on this as well, I encourage any of you to come up as well. Prove my friend to be a liar! Sister Starr, are you a plant?"

"No," Dana said.

"Fine, now come up here and prove that my friend and sister Starr are both liars. And while we are at it, prove me and Magister Wyatt are liars! I defy you to do it!"

Jerry paused at the foot of the stage. "Marcus, you're taking this too far. Your friend has a trick. It's not even a good one. Why are you making..."

"Shut up! Shut up and show us all what charlatans we are."

Jerry shrugged and stepped onto the stage as the room descended into silence.

"Do you have a pen?" Marcus asked.

Jerry patted his pockets and indicated he did not. "Sorry, can I sit down now?"

"Put your wedding ring on the table." Marcus said.

Jerry smirked and said, "Seriously?"

Marcus pointed at the table and glowered at Jerry. Jerry sighed and worked the ring off his finger. He placed it on the table and took a step back.

"Go ahead, Mr. Lane," Magister Wyatt said in a low, calm voice.

Jim effortlessly slid the ring back and forth across the table.

Jerry cocked his head to the side. "There's something with the table, right?"

"No," Jim said.

"Inspect it. To your heart's content," Marcus said.

Jerry looked under the table and ran his hand across the bottom. "Nothing. There's nothing. Can I see your hands?"

Jim held his hands out and Jerry looked them over, searching for something, anything that would explain what he had seen.

"He's clean," Jerry said, turning to the audience. "There's nothing."

Wyatt nodded. "Thank you, Brother Jerry. Don't forget your ring."

The audience murmured. There was still doubt, but it was waning.

"Who else needs evidence? Form a line!"

Seven other Magi took turns, each confirming that they were not plants and that what they had seen was real.

The last one in line presented Jim with a nickel and a plastic cup that had traces of cheap red wine in it. "Ok, let's see how you pull this off, sir," the man said. He placed the nickel on the table and then put the cup upside down over it, creating a red ring on the table. "Now let's see what you can do."

Jim raised his hand, getting bored with the process. He moved it left. Nothing. Then he moved it right and the coin stayed put.

"I can't do it. The cup's in the way," Jim said.

There was some laughter in the audience, and the man who had provided the cup smirked. "I don't know how you did your little trick, but if this cup stops you, well, I guess the magic isn't all that powerful."

"I can't reach through the cup. It's in the way," Jim said, a slight panic in his voice.

"Cute trick," the man said. "You need to work on the presentation, though. What else you got?"

Ally stood up and shouted, "What is wrong with you? That's not a trick, Jim has a gift!"

"Well, miss, his gift just got stopped by a two-cent plastic cup. So, maybe let's not anoint this guy as king of the magicians just yet."

"Are you serious?" Ally asked. "You saw what he did!"

"I just saw what he didn't do."

"Are you insane? Are you blind?" Ally said, shaking.

"Why don't you shut up and let your boyfriend handle this himself. Sit down."

"Enough!" Jim screamed. "I don't care if you believe me or not! I don't have to prove anything to you people. Here, get your nickel."

Jim threw his hands apart with a quick, violent motion. The plastic cup cartwheeled off the table and landed on the floor, clattering on the wood. Jim moved his hands again, and the nickel slid towards the edge slowly. The effect was not as dramatic.

The man's jaw dropped and he stood there in dumb silence.

"Take your nickel," Marcus said in a low, calm voice. "And sit down."

The man took the coin and stalked back to his seat.

"Ashamed!" a voice bellowed from the back of the hall. An old man in a wheelchair was making his way forward. "You should all be ashamed for what you have done here!"

Everyone was silent as the man rolled his way to the edge of the stage. "Young man, I have watched and practiced magic for three of your lifetimes. Never once have I seen someone do what you have done tonight. You have something I have searched for my entire life. You have true magic, and we are all humbled to be in your presence."

The old man looked familiar to Jim, who felt on the verge of collapsing.

"Magister Wyatt, give this boy a golden wand."

"But, sir, he has not gone through the steps to earn it."

"By God, man, what other steps does he need? Give him his wand."

Wyatt nodded and scurried off the stage.

"The rest of you, tell this man you are sorry. Do it and do it now!"

Apologies mixed with a few cheers came from the audience.

The man in the wheelchair looked at Jim. Jim felt nervous. "Most impressive, Mr. Lane," the man said.

"Thank you, Mr. . . . ." Jim started.

"Mel Hall."

"Oh, I grew up watching *Magic Menagerie!*"

"Yes, yes. I know," Hall said with a dismissive gesture. "Son, I am a student of magical history, a fair showman, and was a reasonably skilled practitioner before the years robbed me of that. But you. I've never seen anything like it."

Wyatt walked back on stage, carrying a small, long box.

"Mr. Lane, it is pleasure to offer you membership into the Southern Magi," Wyatt said, opening the box. Inside was a standard magician's wand that had been painted gold. "Most take years to be offered their golden wand. It is an honor, a privilege, and comes with duties. Do you accept?"

Jim looked at Marcus, who nodded.

"Yes, sir," Jim said.

Wyatt nodded solemnly and handed the wand to Jim. "Welcome, Brother Lane, you are one of us!"

The audience erupted into applause. Jim caught Ally's eyes. She gave him a thumbs up.

After general greetings with the members, Mel pulled Jim, Ally, and Marcus into a side room.

"I keep this office here," Mel said waving an arm around the room cluttered with props and old photographs of live performances.

"Marcus," Mel began, "I expect you to keep this young man under your wing."

"Yes, sir, of course," Marcus said.

"Jim, I have something difficult to say to you. Will you hear it?" Mel asked.

Jim nodded.

"I meant what I said out there. You are unique. There's always been stories of people with true magic, but never any proof. You do understand how extraordinary this is, don't you?"

"Yes, sir."

"Ally, this could become very complicated. Do you understand that?"

"Not really, no," she said.

"I was on television for decades, making a living off of tricks for children. Balls and cups. Scarves and top hats. I am respected here because I have a lifetime of knowledge of magic and a modicum of fame. But, if the world somehow were to accept the fact that your boy is truly magical, things would be difficult. He'd be praised by some, decried as a consort of the devil by others."

"Sounds kind of hot," Ally said.

Mel smiled. "Jim, is this the only power you possess? Mind you, it is more than enough, but I am trying to grasp the scope of this."

"No, this is it. I can move light things a little bit."

"Unless someone covers them with a cup, of course," Mel interjected.

"Right," Jim said. "I have to be able to reach them. It's hard to explain."

Mel held up a hand. "No. No. No need to. What about traditional magic tricks and illusions? Can you do them?"

"I have. I can," Jim said.

"Marcus, is that right?" Mel asked.

"Honestly, no. He's terrible at standard magic."

"Ouch," Ally said.

"No, he's right," Jim said.

"Granted I only saw tonight's efforts, but it strikes me that your stage presence is less than, shall we say, polished."

"I haven't done stage magic since high school," Jim said, with a hint of apology.

"What was your skill level at that time?" Mel asked.

"Not great," Jim said.

Mel looked from Ally to Marcus, whose faces confirmed Jim's assessment of his skills. The old man nodded. "Well, what is your plan here?" he asked.

"I don't have one," Jim said.

"Do you hope to take your talents on the road, and capitalize on them?"

"I really haven't given that any thought," Jim said. "Marcus just wanted me to come here tonight to show the Magi what I can do."

"I see. I see," Mel said. "Marcus, what was your thinking?"

"I felt duty bound to let you see real magic," Marcus said. "Beyond that, I was hoping for wise counsel."

"I can offer my counsel. I'll leave it to you to decide if it is wise," Mel said, fixing his eyes on Jim. "Jim, do you want my advice?"

"Yes, sir."

"You have a rare, probably unique, talent. But that talent is, for lack of a better word . . . boring. Sure, it's a miracle, but it's got no sizzle," Mel said. "And, frankly, Jim, neither do you."

"Okay, now look. You have no right to talk to him that way," Ally said, her arms crossed.

"Hear me out," Mel said, holding up a liver spotted hand. "I am old, so I get to speak my mind, and I long ago realized that it's better to speak plainly and hurt someone's feelings if it will prevent greater pain later."

Ally frowned at Mel, but offered no further argument.

"Your talent is such that anyone who paid to see it would feel they had not spent their money well," Mel continued. "It's such a small miracle, isn't it? No flash, no pop, nothing that would captivate an audience, do you see?"

"I do, yes," Jim said.

"And because it is so simple, people won't think much of it. Of course, no one will think it's real magic. That doesn't exist, right?" Mel said.

Jim began to speak, but Mel cut him off.

"Those of us in this room know it's real, but the average Tom, Dick, or Harriet won't ever believe it is," Mel said.

"What about the people that were in that auditorium, they believed it by the time he was done," Ally said.

"That's true. If you ask them now, they'll say they saw real magic," Mel said. "But ask them again tomorrow. They'll have convinced themselves they were taken in by a well-executed trick. Nobody's brain is going to let them believe they saw an honest to God wizard."

"So, what are you suggesting?" Ally asked, an edge still in her voice.

"I suggest you don't perform in public," Mel said, his eyes boring into Jim's. "Unless, that is, you put together an act where you surround your true magic with the kind of mumbo jumbo the rest of us trade in. And, from what I'm hearing and seeing, I just don't think that's going to happen."

Jim pursed his lips and inhaled through his nose.

"You know he's right, Jim," Marcus said. "You can't just do what you can do."

"Yeah. He is," Jim said. "Mr. Hall, thank you."

"I just owed it to you to speak my mind."

Jim nodded.

"But, look," Mel said. "There's no reason not to practice. Maybe you can make this thing stronger. Maybe you can, against all odds, become good at fake magic too. Who knows? Marcus, will you keep an eye on Jim and help him as you can?"

"Of course. Anytime I am in town, I am at your disposal," Marcus said with a slight, formal bow towards Jim.

"Alright. Good," Mel said with a wave of his hands. "Jim, it is an honor to meet you. You are truly more special than anyone who has ever made his way into this building, even if you never set foot on stage again."

***

Marcus went back on the road two days later. He had a series of shows throughout the Midwest, and would be back in town in five months, when he had a week of shows at The Diamond Sun, one of the casinos in Tunica, Mississippi, about an hour outside of Memphis.

Jim promised Marcus he would practice in his absence. Even with Ally's patient assistance, neither his skills nor his act improved. Marcus checked in as often as he could, but there was little he could say or do from the road to help Jim.

Ally and Jim fell back into their normal routines and stayed in touch with their friends. A month before Marcus was scheduled to return for his Tunica gig, Stan Huang moved back to Memphis. His mother was ill, and the company he was working for had just been bought out by a larger competitor. "It's the universe talking, I guess," Stan said.

He had another job with a local operation within three weeks, and his mother's health improved. The company that bought out Stan's old employer laid off over half the workforce in Arizona.

Nick graduated law school. In mid-October, he learned he had passed the bar exam. He went to work with the firm in Oxford where he had been clerking.

When Marcus returned, he was disappointed to see for himself that what Jim had told him was accurate. Jim's act and progress were non-existent. Marcus tried to be positive and encouraging, and procured VIP comps to his show in Tunica for Jim and Ally. When he heard Stan was in town, Marcus expressed concerns that he would tell everyone in a three-state area about Jim's abilities. Jim assured him he had not told Stan anything.

"Jim is a wizard, not an idiot," Ally added.

Marcus was pleased to hear this, and made sure that Stan got a VIP package as well.

Stan hitched a ride to Tunica with Ally and Jim for the show. The drive was punctuated with awkward patches as Jim and Ally considered telling Stan their secret. They managed to keep their counsel, but the pauses did not go unnoticed. Stan assumed they were either getting married, that Ally was pregnant, or a combination thereof.

As they pulled into the parking lot of The Diamond Sun, an electronic billboard with Marcus' face greeted them with a scrolling banner that read "NOW LIVE: The Magic of Marco Blade (as seen on TV)."

"Our man has made it!" shouted Stan "Name in lights and everything!"

"And, he has been seen on TV, so there's that," Ally said.

Casinos in Tunica are only allowed to operate if they are floating on the Mississippi River. But, this is one of the most twisted legal technicalities on the books. The casinos are built on barges, which are then permanently affixed to docks. From the outside, there is absolutely no indication that they are boats, and, indeed, it is hard to imagine these facilities somehow chugging down the river while a lookout stands watch bellowing "Mark Twain!" from time to time. Indeed, even the whole concept of the casinos being on the river is a legal fiction. Yes, the water they are on comes from the mighty Mississippi, but not by natural design. Crews dug channels to create fake waterways on which multimillion-dollar casino/hotels pretend to float, all to appease a certain segment of the population that is a little more comfortable with their sin being offshore than on.

The exterior of the Diamond Sun was meant to conjure the idea of a wild west saloon, but it just looked like a giant brown block with neon sign lettering evocative of a

Tombstone brothel. Inside, the casino was filled with an odd combination of smoke and people wheeling around their own oxygen supplies. The path from the front door to the showroom meandered past loud slot machines, tables full of people counting to 21, and boisterous craps pits.

Stan suggested they stop for a few minutes at one of the craps tables. "I don't know how to play," Jim said, looking at the erupting chaos and the placard that stated there was a $10 minimum bet.

"I can teach you," Stan said. "It's fun. And you can yell a lot."

"Maybe after the show, guys," Ally said. "We only have a few minutes."

Jim agreed, as did Stan, albeit begrudgingly. They made their way to the showroom, which was like a Vegas venue, but with folding chairs and somewhat rattier black velvet drapes lining the walls than you might find adorning showrooms on the Strip. They sat at one of the few tables near the front in the Diamond Club VIP area. A waitress informed them that their package included two beers each. Domestic.

Beat for beat, the show was the same one Ally and Jim had seen at the University the year before. Still, they properly complimented the amazing Marco Blade afterwards. Stan, who had not been at the earlier show, asked a lot of questions about the levitation effects with a mixture of curiosity and jealousy.

Marcus agreed to meet the trio for dinner after his late show. The casino boasted that it had three distinct dining options. A snack bar selling "Delta Dawgs" and "Dixie Chicken" sandwiches, made from frozen patties and slapped in a microwave oven. There was also the *Ten Carat Buffet*, which offered industrial sized servings of dressed up cafeteria fare. On Saturdays, the star of the show was overcooked and desiccated prime rib. On Fridays, there were surprisingly decent crab legs. Other nights were a hit or miss mélange of standard ethnic and/or fried foods along with a surprising variety of potato options. Finally, discerning diners and high rollers could enjoy "Miss Ruby's Steakhouse," which was high quality and equally high priced. Fortunately, because of Marcus' celebrity status, he could join them there. More importantly, they could enjoy a meal for free.

While they waited for Marcus, Stan insisted on providing a craps lesson. Ally and Jim agreed. At first, they watched Stan place bets on the bewildering table layout as people chucked dice, leading to cheers or lamentations from around the oblong table. After about 20 minutes, and the requisite jokes from Ally regarding the difference between the "Come" and "Don't Come" lines as well as quips about the "hard way" bets, she bought in for $100. Jim provided moral support.

Ally waited her turn as three shooters went before her with various degrees of success eliciting various responses around the table ranging from shouts of joy to salty lamentations of despair. Ultimately the sevens caught them all.

The stickman slid the dice across the green felt layout to Ally, and said with faux enthusiasm "Next shooter!" Ally froze up until Stan told her to put $10 on the Come line, which made her smirk before she dropped two red chips. She picked up the dice in her right hand. "Wish me luck, babe," she said to Jim.

Jim obliged, patting her on the back. "Knock 'em dead."

Ally shook the translucent red dice in her right hand and flung them down the pit. The dice bounced and careened off the gray foam rubber interior wall before they stopped, revealing a two and a six.

Following Stan's instructions, she backed her original bet, as the stickman pushed the dice to her again.

"So, I need an eight before I get a seven, right?" she asked Stan, who nodded with the look of a proud teacher.

Ally scooped up the dice and chucked them down the table.

"Four. Hard way, four," the stickman called out as the crew shuffled chips around the table. A couple of people at the far end were celebrating their good fortune for having won an absolute sucker bet.

"This is fun," Ally said.

"It'll be more fun when you win," Jim said.

The dice came back to Ally and she grabbed them, giving them a couple of quick shakes before rolling them down the green cloth.

The dice bounced off the far wall. For a moment, it looked like they were going to end up a six and one, but at the last moment, the one tipped over to a two.

"Eight. Winner, eight!" the stickman called out, pushing a small stack of chips to Ally's position.

Ally shouted and hugged Jim, before high fiving Stan.

The players around the table started placing their bets for the new round.

"Ok, let's go," Jim said.

"She can't go now! She's still up!" Stan said. "Besides, you're having fun. I think your voodoo helped her win, Jim!"

"Voodoo?" Ally asked.

"Yeah, he did this weird little hand motion right before the dice landed," Stan said, wiggling his fingers to demonstrate. "I guess it worked!"

Ally looked at Jim, who decided it was the appropriate time to really get to know the intricate pattern on the carpeting.

Ally took a breath, and turned back to the craps table. "Cash me out," she said in a cool, flat voice.

***

"You guys are messing with me. Messing with me super hard," Stan said.

"They are not," Marcus said, cutting a piece of steak. "The reality is that they are messing more with me, isn't that right, Jim?"

"I'm not messing with anyone," Jim said, taking a sip of wine. He waved his hand and moved a butter pat off his bread plate.

"What are you doing, man!" Marcus said in a voice that was arguably a whisper.

"Magic," Jim said. "I'm doing magic."

Stan slapped the table. "Damn! I don't even know what to say."

"Maybe we should all stop saying anything, at least while we are in the casino, okay?" Ally said.

"It's okay, babe," Jim said. "It's just a little mystic mumbo jumbo, yeah?"

"Magic. Felony. It's a thin line, hon," Ally said.

"Okay, okay, let us all keep our composure," Marcus said, looking around the high-end steakhouse. Couples and groups sat in the dimly lit room that was a little too consciously trying to recreate the exclusive atmosphere of an early 1960's joint where Sinatra might have thrown back a double of Jack while digging into some prime beef. No one was paying attention to them.

"Ally's point is well taken," Marcus continued when he looked back at them. "We probably should not discuss this here at all, much less in such animated tones, agreed?"

Everyone muttered in the affirmative.

"The important thing is that it doesn't happen again," Marcus said, pointing a fork dramatically at the other three before cracking a smile. "Or, at least that it be done with more thought."

"Wait, what are you saying, Marcus?" Ally asked.

"What I'm saying is that if you go down this road, be smart about it and it may be a way to make a career out of magic."

"Get rich, son!" Stan said. "This steak is amazing, by the way."

"Hold on, boys," Ally said. "You aren't seriously suggesting Jim makes a habit out of cheating, are you?"

"There is no law against the use of magic, is there?"

"Not that I'm aware of," said Jim. "Maybe we should call Nick and get a consultation on this."

He paused as the others looked at him before he started laughing.

"No, you guys are right. Nick probably doesn't specialize in magic law. Man, that might be a good fantasy series, don't you think. A wizard who is a lawyer for other wizards? I'd read that," Jim said, pouring more wine into his glass.

"How many is that?" Ally asked.

"Enough for me to think a wizard lawyer is hilarious," Jim said.

"Legal technicalities aside, I am sure there are issues to consider." Marcus said. "Obviously, I can't involve myself with this sort of thing. Which means you can't show up and do this when I'm performing, right?"

"Don't worry, Marcus, we aren't going to do this again, right?" Ally asked.

Everyone looked to Jim.

"I don't know. It's magic. It's probably not illegal. It feels kind of like a heist movie but without guns."

"Jim, I don't...." Ally said.

"Come on, Ally, you gotta be kidding me. If Jim can do this, what's the downside?" Stan asked.

"It just feels weird," she said.

"It's pretty weird," Jim said.

"It also seems like it'd be a good way to make some jack," Stan said.

"We won't get greedy, right?" Ally said, swirling wine in her glass.

"No," Jim said. "Not too greedy."

"A little greedy though?" Stan asked hopefully.

"Just a little," Jim said. "Maybe enough for a down payment on a house."

Ally smiled. "That might be nice."

**

For the next few weeks, Jim and Ally practiced manipulating dice. They started by tossing the dice in a shoebox before settling on the idea of just lining the dining room table with stacks of books to emulate a craps pit.

Some nights Stan would drop by to offer his advice, encouragement, and to point out the various items they would soon be able to buy once they were rich. Marcus joined sporadically, helping Jim learn that it was easiest to affect a die when it was on the bounce. The trick was to only slightly nudge it so that there was only a minor change. The consensus was that Jim shouldn't flip a die from a 1 to a 6. It had to be a subtle alteration, making the die tumble from one face to an adjacent one.

Marcus and Stan visited the Tuesday after Thanksgiving. By that time, Jim had gained decent proficiency in the manipulation, but was still only hitting the number he wanted about half the time, and then only if the die caught a good bounce.

"Do not get discouraged," Marcus said. "Just keep practicing. I am leaving town for the next month, and have great expectations for you upon my return!"

"Where's the gig?" Ally asked.

"On the fifteenth, I start a week of shows at a riverboat casino in Indiana," Marcus said. "But I leave tomorrow for a meeting on the West Coast. My agent wants me to meet some people in the City of Angels."

"Like, movie people?" Stan asked.

"Television, actually," Marcus said. "No one should hold their breath. It's just a meeting. My agent wants me to get out there. Not a big deal. At least not as of yet."

"That's great, man," Jim said.

"Whatever it is, you got it, Hollywood," Ally said.

"Thank you," Marcus said. "Jim, have you given any thought of how you plan to roll this out?"

"Not really. I assume we have to come up with a way to do it so that the casinos don't know what we are doing."

"We go in as a crew!" Stan said. "Here's what we do. We all arrive separately. I arrive first. I'll be loud and distracting. Win or lose as normal, yeah? After about twenty minutes, Ally rolls in. She'll be our primary shooter. I'll keep being a distraction. After about ten minutes, Jim, you show up. You pretend like you don't know us, and hang back doing your thing. We try to win about 80% of the time, so we do lose some. It'll throw off the security cameras. The casino won't know what hit them!"

"You've put some thought into this, Stan," Ally said.

"I have no life. It's okay."

"So, wait, when I show up, who do I help?" Jim asked.

"Mainly Ally. Sometimes me. We hit 'em for twenty-five grand the first night, then we split. We leave separately, of course."

"So, we need to take three cars down there?" Jim asked.

"Yes. We don't want to get made in the parking lot."

"When did you become a secondary Scorsese character?" Ally asked.

"Oh, you think I'm funny?" Stan said, trying to look mean. It just made everyone laugh.

"That sounds entertaining and all," Marcus said. "But how about you just go in and play. Jim do your thing. Leave when you hit a goal. Twenty-five grand may be ambitious for day one. Try a little lower your first night. Maybe five-thousand."

"But won't they get suspicious?" Jim asked.

"Probably, but what are they going to do? Call the police and report a case of malicious wizardry?" Marcus asked.

"I don't know. We probably need some cover," Jim said.

"Jim. Just use your ability. They can't prove it, and I am not aware of it even being a crime to do magic," Marcus said.

"There's a few ladies from Salem that may take issue with that," Ally said.

***

Ally, Jim and Stan continued to practice over the next few weeks. By the time Marcus got home (without any solid news of an onramp to stardom), Jim's accuracy had increased to about 75%, where it stalled out. They all agreed it was good enough.

They decided it was a good idea that Marcus refrain from joining them due to what they all agreed was his "almost celebrity status." However, much to Stan's chagrin, Jim and Ally – mainly Ally – decided it made absolutely no sense for them to travel alone to Tunica or to stagger their entrance into the casino. The day after Christmas, Ally and Jim drove down to Tunica. Stan insisted on driving separately because he wanted to enter the casino at a different time from the other two despite the fact they all agreed there was a low risk of being caught cheating, if what they were going to do was even technically cheating.

Jim and Ally pulled up on the large blacktop parking lot that the Diamond Sun shared with The Lucky Shamrock, another casino.

"You ready for this?" Ally asked Jim as they stood by the car, looking at the Diamond Sun.

"I guess. It's just – Well are we sure this is right?"

"No," Ally said. "But I'm not sure it's wrong. It's just something no one could anticipate, right? Maybe value neutral."

"Can't argue with neutral values," Jim said.

"Come on, let's go have some fun."

Ally and Jim walked into the casino. Jim nervously greeted the security officers at the front door, convinced they had already made him as a master thief. Ally guided him past the initial bank of loud, flashing slot machines and their primarily mirthless players to the table games. They spotted Stan at a craps table, where he was tossing dice and making a good bit of noise.

"Ten. Gimme a ten!" he shouted tossing the dice down the table. The dice and the pit crew promptly informed him he had hit a seven, and had lost.

Ally took an open spot at the table and Jim stood behind her. She smiled at Stan, who gave her a discrete nod and a not so discrete gesture with his forefinger across his nose, which he had picked up from a late-night viewing of *The Sting* on one of the local channels when he was younger.

Ally bought $200 worth of chips, and waited until the dice came around to her before she placed a $10 wager. Ally took the dice and chucked them down the table. After the bounce, she had a nine. Ally backed up her bet with odds and threw again. They agreed that Jim would not do his thing unless it looked like a seven was imminent. She rolled an eight.

The stickman slid the dice back to her, and she picked them up, gave them a quick shake and threw them down the green felt layout. Jim watched the dice and flicked his hand just before they landed.

"Seven out!" one of the table crew announced, and the stickman pushed the dice to the next shooter. Ally looked at Jim, who shrugged. A couple of shooters later, Stan took the dice. He rolled a four. He looked at Jim, who nodded at him. This time when Jim flicked his fingers, the dice hit Stan's number.

Before Stan's run ended, Jim had made three adjustments, and Stan was up $500, earning cheers from the other players huddled around the table along the way.

About fifteen minutes later, Ally got the dice again. This time, Jim nailed the number six times before she crapped out. She was up $1,000.

By the time the dice made their way around the table two more times, Stan had raked in $2,000, and Ally accumulated $1,500. After her third turn with the dice, Ally looked at Jim, who nodded to her. She requested that her chips be colored up. She and Jim left the table, and cashed out before heading immediately to the exit.

They walked to the car without talking. Jim was feeling shaky, and Ally had decided that a quick, quiet exfiltration was the wisest approach. As they reached the car, someone behind them shouted in a thick Southern accent, "Freeze! You're under arrest!"

They stopped in their tracks, and slowly turned around and saw Stan with an ear-to-ear grin.

Ally immediately punched him in the arm.

"What is wrong with you?" she asked.

"What isn't?" Stan asked.

"Not cool, Stan," Jim said. "I'm close to a coronary as it is."

"Well, at least you can pay your deductible with the winnings!" Stan said.

"I thought we were going to split up," Jim said.

"No one's watching us. We didn't win that much. Not enough for the casino to care."

Ally nodded. "Fair point."

"But next time, we'll be more careful. Because we'll hit them for more. A lot more," Stan said.

"We should probably wait," Jim said.

"I agree. So, how's tomorrow?" Stan asked.

"So soon?" Ally asked. "That doesn't seem . . ."

"And we go for twenty-five grand. Each. It's easy."

"We should wait," Jim said.

"For what?" Stan asked. "Let's knock this out in a few nights; it'll make for a happy new year!"

Jim looked at Ally. She paused before saying, "What the hell. 'Tis the season."

The next night started off much like the previous evening's endeavors. Stan was already playing when Ally and Jim arrived. Jim's accuracy rate was high. Before too long Stan and Ally were both up over two grand. A pit boss approached them separately, and offered to enroll them in the casino's awards program. They agreed and were both issued gold-colored plastic cards within a few minutes, after the boss began a quick entry to start tracking their play. In addition to the cards, they both received buffet vouchers.

Before the hour was up, Ally and Stan had hit their twenty-five thousand dollar goals. Ally decided to cash out. She and Jim agreed that they'd save the buffet voucher for another time.

As they walked out of the casino, Tonya Henderson, the Diamond Sun's head of security was reviewing the footage from the craps table they had been playing on. She immediately determined that Ally, Jim and Stan knew each other. That was easy. She pulled up Ally and Stan's play records. Nothing before tonight. They had both made a lot of money too quickly, and it didn't add up. She noticed Jim behind Ally, and took note of the fact that he never played. Jim's hand motions didn't register with her. She thought maybe there was something going on with the dice. She sent an officer to pull the dice from the table for inspection, and kept watching. Within twenty minutes she was satisfied that there was nothing amiss with the dice and could not think of any way the three could be cheating.

She did not know who Jim was, as he did not have a rewards card, but she put a note in the system to keep an eye on Ally and Stan if they returned.

***

"We should stop," Jim said on the ride home.

"Probably," Ally agreed. "We've made a lot. If you're uncomfortable, babe, we can quit."

"It's not that I'm uncomfortable, really," Jim said. "I just, I don't know, feel like I shouldn't be using the magic for this."

"I get it. I do," Ally said, staring out at the passing flat countryside. "If you want to stop, let's stop. Or, if you want, we can do one more. Pull in enough to make a bigger down payment on a house."

"Yeah," said Jim nodding. "With maybe enough left over to pay for a wedding?"

"Is that a proposal?" Ally asked.

"I suppose it is."

Ally burst into laughter. "It sucked! We're driving on a Mississippi highway and you didn't even give me a ring. This is not the way this sort of thing usually goes down."

"So, that's a no?" Jim asked.

"Of course, it's not, you idiot," Ally said. "It's a definite yes. But I still want a ring."

"Then let's come back one more time and win you one," Jim said.

Ally leaned over and kissed Jim on the cheek. "Sounds like a plan, fiancée."

***

The crew returned two nights later. There was some discussion about switching casinos, but Stan pointed out that they could earn rewards at the Diamond Sun. Stan's argument that centered on "Free steak!" combined with what seemed like the impossibility of being caught led the group to decide they would continue to patronize the same joint.

Stan again showed up early, and handed his rewards card to the pit boss, who dutifully logged him in. This triggered an alert in the security control room. Tonya Henderson made sure that all the cameras on and around the pit were on her view screen and confirmed they were all functional and recording. Tonya received another ping when Ally checked in a few minutes later. The security chief cycled through the four relevant camera views, keeping an eye out for – well she wasn't sure what.

Tonya watched as Ally took the dice and tossed them. Eight came up on the roll. Tonya zoomed the camera to get as clear a view of Ally's hands as she could. Ally shook the dice and threw them again. Tonya turned her attention to another camera to watch the dice bounce off the pit wall and land on the felt. She got an eight. Eight is an easy point, Tonya thought, but something bothered her. She rewound the video and it appeared that there was a weird little shudder with one of the dice. One die – the normal one – landed normally on a five. But the other one seemed to teeter on landing on a two, but at the last moment took a weird little bounce so that it hit three.

Tonya pushed a button. "Pit four, swap out the dice. Send the old ones to me."

Moments later, Tonya watched her monitors and saw a man in a suit approach the stickman, who promptly scooped the dice out of the layout, and replaced them with a new set.

Tonya watched as Ally picked up the fresh dice. Ally shook the dice; there was nothing unusual with her movements and no indication of any kind of swap out. She threw the dice and hit a seven on the come out. Everything looked normal. She rolled again and got a nine. She threw again, and hit a hard eight. Again, nothing seemed amiss. She tossed again, and this time the dice took an odd little jittery hop before landing on seven, ending her roll. But something about the bounce seemed off somehow. Tonya couldn't place it, but kept her eye on the camera.

Within a few minutes, Tonya had the old dice. She inspected them, and saw nothing off. No loads. No magnets. Nothing but dice. She sent them for destructive inspection, but knew that would reveal nothing. Still, she had to perform her due diligence.

A couple of shooters later, Stan took the dice. Tonya watched closely, and everything played out normally for the first couple of tosses. Then she saw one of the dice do that odd shimmy before giving Stan his point. Nothing on the video revealed evidence of cheating. She rewound and watched it repeatedly.

Tonya switched the feed and scrutinized Ally during Stan's roll. She wasn't doing anything unusual. On her third rewind of the video on Ally, her focus switched to Jim. She noticed him wave his hand as the dice bounced off the pit wall. She pulled up the camera trained on the dice, and displayed it side by side with the one focusing on Ally and Jim. As she thought, the hand movement was in sync with the odd bounce of the dice. She laughed. Players often tried to use the Force to alter the roll of the dice. Nothing strange about that.

But something nagged at her. She rewound to Ally's turn. Sure enough, the man behind her was doing the Jedi mind trick on the dice when Ally hit her number. He also did it on the roll that bounced oddly, but made her seven out. Again, that wouldn't be so weird. Players do goofy stuff. But what was bugging Tonya was that he didn't do it every roll. Just on the ones where the dice behaved strangely.

"Frank, cover the monitors. Keep an eye on pit four. I'm hitting the floor," she said.

"Sure, boss," Frank said. "We got a problem?"

"We got something," Tonya said. "But hell if I know what it is."

By the time Tonya made her way to the floor, Ally had about $30,000 in the rack in front of her. Stan had almost as much. Tonya walked into the pit, grabbed a clipboard and pretended to write. She waited until the dice came back around to Ally. Ally established a six on her come out roll. On her second throw, a five came up. The dice tumbled normally, and Tonya observed that Jim didn't make any motions. On the third roll, the dice jittered ever so slightly, and what was almost a seven landed on six, leading to cheers all around the table. Tonya noticed that Jim had waved his fingers just before the dice did their weird little dance.

After hitting three points, Ally lost.

Tonya kept watching. Every time – every single time – the dice made a strange movement on Ally or Stan's roll, Jim had made his motion. Tonya inspected and replaced the dice again. Finding nothing wrong, the game continued.

After about thirty minutes, and nearly a dozen instances of dancing dice and waving fingers, Ally's chip total was approaching $60,000. A pit boss had already given her and Stan steakhouse and room vouchers. Tonya was losing her patience. Ally put $10,000 on the Come line, rolled the dice, and hit a four. She rolled again, and as the dice landed, Jim waved. The dice tumbled, jittered and the dice faces showed a one and a three. Another winner.

Tonya walked to the table and whispered to the stickman. He nodded and passed the dice to the next shooter.

"It's still my turn," Ally said.

"Color her up. And the gentleman at position five," Tonya said pointing to Stan. "Time for you to call it an evening."

Stan looked at Ally, as the other players offered their opinion of the situation to the crew. Once their chips were colored up and handed to them, Tonya said, "Thank you both, now let my associates and I help you cash those out. Follow me, please. You too," she said gesturing at Jim, as two security officers approached the table.

Ally, Jim, and Stan stood in place for a moment.

"Now, please," Tonya said.

The three followed Tonya, and the two security officers walked behind them. They passed bank of cashiers' cages, which prompted Stan to say, "We can cash out here, yeah?"

Tonya kept walking, and the security officers behind them nudged the group on. Ally looked at Jim. "Don't panic," she whispered, almost convincingly.

"This can't be good," Stan said.

Tonya reached a locked door and waved her ID in front of a scanner. The magnetic lock on the door release, and she opened it, holding it for the group.

"Through here, please," she said.

The group nervously passed through the doorway. The carpet turned into industrial school-grade linoleum, and the garish décor of the casino disappeared in favor of white painted cinderblock walls. After they made their way into the hall, Tonya led them past several closed, windowless doors and took a left turn when the hall created a t-intersection. She led them down the hall and unlocked a door, ushering them inside a Spartan office. Two folding chairs faced a simple desk. Two more folding chairs were parked against a side wall.

"Please have a seat," Tonya said.

"I think I'd rather leave," Stan said.

"You can do that, Mr. Huang" Tonya said. "But you may get detoured on your way home by the Tunica County Sheriff's Office."

"So, are we under arrest for something," Jim asked.

"Not yet, sir," Tonya said. "But I wonder why you'd ask a question like that. Now, if you three don't mind, just sit tight for a moment, and I'll be back, okay?"

"Can we make a call?" Ally asked.

"Knock yourself out, Ms. Barnes." Tonya said as she left the office with the two security offices, shutting the door behind her.

Stan went to the door and tried to turn the knob. They were locked in.

Ally pulled out her cell phone, pulled up her contacts and tried to make a call. There was no cell service.

"Who are you trying to call?" Jim asked.

"The only lawyer I know in the great state of Mississippi – Nick. I got no bars in this bunker."

"Try the landline," Stan said.

Ally picked up the desk phone, and instinctively dialed 9 before the number she had for Nick in her contacts. After two rings, Nick picked up. Ally explained their predicament, leaving out some salient details. Nick advised her to stay calm and to not answer any questions, and said he'd be there within an hour with one of his partners.

Fifteen minutes later Tonya returned. "Well, how did you do it?"

"Do what?" Stan asked.

"Take over one hundred grand from my casino."

"Luck," Stan said.

"Yeah, not buying that," Tonya said.

"I don't care . . ." Stan started, before Ally interrupted him.

"Is there a particular reason we should answer your questions?"

"Ms. Barnes, you can answer my questions or you can talk to the Sheriff down at the jail. I'm much nicer," Tonya said.

"We're good, thanks," Ally said.

"Do you all feel that way?" Tonya asked.

Stan smirked. Jim stared at the floor. Neither said a word.

"Okay, then," Tonya said. "I'll be back."

She left, once again locking the door behind her.

"What are we going to do?" Jim asked.

"Not freak out," Stan said. "And remember they've probably got this room wired for sound, so let's keep it cool."

They sat in silence for another half hour before Tonya returned. She tried to get them to talk again to no avail before she gave up and locked them in the office again.

An hour and a half after they arrived in the office, the door opened again. This time, two security officers came in with Nick, who was wearing a jacket and white button down shirt with no tie and a couple of buttons undone at the top.

The group stood up to greet him, and he held up a hand.

"I'm going to let my partner do the talking."

"Why thank you, Nicholas," a deep, Southern voice said from the hallway just before a man wearing a charcoal grey suit and tie, and sporting a mustache and goatee walked in, a black walking stick tapping on the floor. "It is the thing that I am best suited for."

Wyatt Taylor entered the room and looked around, his eyes locking in on Jim's. Jim took a deep breath, and Wyatt shook his head.

"Well, well, well, what have we here?" Wyatt asked. "What did this band of desperados allegedly do?"

"I'll tell you what they did," Tonya said as she made her way into the room, having obviously run to the office. "They robbed this casino."

"Strong words," Wyatt said. "I assume we have ironclad proof on that point."

"We have video, yes," Tonya said.

"What crime have you captured? Armed robbery, rigged deck or dice? Some elaborate heist, perhaps?"

"Counselor, these people cheated. End of story," Tonya said.

"Sounds more like the beginning if you ask me," Wyatt said.

"Can you tell us what you are alleging," Nick asked. "Maybe show us this video you supposedly have."

Tonya glared at the lawyers. "Alright, let me show you some video."

The Chief of Security moved to the desk and logged into the computer. She pulled up the security camera and showed Nick and Wyatt a series of videos.

"Watch the dice on camera two and then watch Mr. Lane of three," Tonya said as she cycled through several videos of the group.

"Looks like the lady and the other gentleman here had some good luck," Wyatt said. "I'm not aware of the casino industry criminalizing that, try as you might."

"Watch Mr. Lane," Tonya said. "See what he does with his hand. Watch the dice when he does it."

She showed them multiple instances where Jim used his abilities to alter the outcome of the dice.

"What's your point?" Nick asked.

"Every time your client moved his hands, the dice moved oddly. Almost every time, Ms. Barnes' and Mr. Huang's dice hit their point," Tonya said.

"Are you suggesting that Mr. Lane has a transmitter, or that your dice are being remotely controlled," Nick asked.

"No," Tonya said with a hesitation. "The dice are clean."

"So, what are you claiming?" Nick asked.

"Your clients must be cheating. Do you know what the odds are of a bunch of green players hitting numbers with that frequency?" Tonya asked.

"Well, I suppose that is why they call them odds," Wyatt said with a smile. "Because they can just be so darn odd, can they not?"

Jim, Ally, and Stan sat quietly. Jim tried to avoid eye contact with Wyatt, which was not problematic, as the lawyer was avoiding looking at his clients.

"You have to admit there's something messed up here," Tonya said.

"I admit nothing," Wyatt said. "You've already told me there was not a thing wrong with the dice. That being the case, it seems – and I feel ridiculous even saying this out loud – but it seems like you may be accusing my client of using some kind of witchcraft on the dice. Does that sum it up?"

"Well, no . . ." Tonya started.

"What then?" Wyatt asked.

"I don't know," Tonya said.

"So, you have no evidence of wrongdoing, but you think it's possible my client is using arcane power," Wyatt said, before fixing his gaze on Jim. "I am sure that if Mr. Lane were a wizard, he would not use his powers to affect a craps game in rural Mississippi. That would be a most grievous misuse of such a power, wouldn't it?"

Wyatt looked directly at Jim, pausing for a moment. "Most grievous."

"In any event," Wyatt said, turning his attention back to Tonya, "assuming arguendo that dark sorcery is off the table, it sounds like you have no evidence or plausible explanation to support any kind of malfeasance on the part of my clients. I have that right, don't I?"

Tonya did not respond.

"I see," Wyatt said, drumming his fingers on his walking stick. "If you have nothing more than the nothing you appear to have, I strongly suggest you end this nonsense and let my clients cash out their winnings."

"I think we'll hold onto their chips," Tonya said.

Jim and Ally looked at each other. Stan said something colorful.

Wyatt held up his hand. "You will do no such thing. You have no indication of cheating. Also, I bet if I ask these three if they were willing guests here they would tell me they were not."

"They locked us in!" Stan nearly shouted.

"Mr. Parson, what does that sound like to you?" Wyatt asked.

"False imprisonment," Nick said.

"False imprisonment!" Wyatt said, slamming his walking stick on the industrial tile floor. "Nasty ring, that. I assume you don't want us suing for the improperly withheld winnings plus false imprisonment. Could be ugly. Very ugly."

Tonya exhaled and looked at the security officers. "Please escort these good people to the cages and let them cash out. Then make sure they promptly leave the property."

She looked back towards the three. "You are no longer welcome at this casino. I wouldn't bother going to any of the other casinos either. You three have made the list. Show up here again, and you will be arrested. For real," Tonya said.

"I can do that, can't I counselor?"

"Indeed, you can," Wyatt said. "Well, let's wrap this little soiree up, shall we?"

"Go on," Tonya said, and marched out of the room. The security officers walked the group to a cashiers' cage and followed them to the casino's front entrance when that business was complete.

Stan and Ally each had checks in excess of $100,000 in their pockets.

"Thank you for helping us Nick and Mr. Taylor," Stan said. "That was scary."

"Don't mention it, son," Wyatt said. "If you have any trouble cashing the checks – which you shouldn't – you let Nick know and we'll take care of it. Now, Nick, why don't you walk with Mr. Huang to his car so I can speak to these two, gather contact information and what not."

Nick agreed and walked across the asphalt with Stan.

"Thank you again," Jim said to Wyatt.

"The Southern Order's next meeting is in two weeks," Wyatt said flatly. "You will be there, and I will make sure Marcus is also present. This is not an invitation. This is a requirement. Am I clear?"

"You can't talk to us like that," Ally said.

"I can. I did. And I will again. Frankly, Ms. Barnes, this does not concern you. You are welcome to attend. Or not, I honestly don't care. But Jim, you will be there. Am I clear?"

"You are."

Wyatt nodded, then turned and walked away.

"Don't worry about it, babe," Ally said. "What are they going to do, burn you at the stake?"

"I'm not ruling that out," Jim said.

***

When Jim and Ally arrived at the Southern Magi's meeting two weeks later, they were greeted at the door by Derrick again. This time the tall doorkeeper did not exchange pleasantries. He just asked them to follow him into the auditorium. As they walked through the lounge. The members either avoided eye contact or shook their heads as they passed. Only one person – the girl with purple hair – smiled at them.

Derrick guided Jim and Ally to chairs in the auditorium.

The night they were ousted from the casino, Jim had called Marcus and left a voicemail. The next day, Marcus called him back. When Jim explained everything that had happened, Marcus without hesitation said he would fly back to town for the meeting. When Jim asked him if the situation was bad, Marcus had simply told him, "Well, it's not good."

A few uncomfortable minutes later, Marcus was led in and sat next to Jim and Ally. "Thank you for coming, Marcus," Jim said.

Marcus looked over at him and nodded. "Maybe we don't talk until this is over."

Jim nodded and the three of them sat quietly as the Southern Magi began to file into the room. None spoke to them, and the seats near them remained empty.

After everyone settled in and settled down, Wyatt made his way to the stage.

"We shall dispense with the usual order of business and get right down to why we are here. I hereby convene this hearing to expel Magus James Lane and Magus Marcus Wade from the Order for the wanton misuse of magic in the furtherance of a criminal scheme."

Jim tried to whisper to Marcus, who waved him away.

For the next twenty minutes, Wyatt set forth the case against Jim and Marcus. His description of what happened was surprisingly accurate and detailed. It was also very effective. Throughout the presentation, there were outbursts of shock and recrimination from the caped cadre of magicians in the audience. Jim and Marcus could practically feel the heat of the hateful stares aimed their way.

Wyatt wrapped up his presentation, punctuating his comments with the occasional fist to the lectern.

"We cannot, must not, tolerate members who misuse their talents – natural or not – to swindle or steal. It is, therefore, my request that the Southern Magi revoke the memberships of Marcus Wade and James Lane. The latter for using his skills to steal. The former for giving him the guidance to do so," Wyatt said to the crowd before turning directly to Jim and Marcus "The Southern Magi do not benefit from such behavior, and these gentlemen no longer deserve their wands."

A hush fell over the audience. Wyatt nodded. "Do either of you have anything you want to say before we vote?"

Marcus rose to his feet. "Magister, I take full responsibility. Jim was under my tutelage, and I let him and the Order down. But, this situation is unique, and I use that word as it is truly intended to be used. Never before, and never again, will an issue like this arise. I merely ask that the Order show some mercy and kindness."

"Mr. Lane, do you have anything to say for yourself?" Wyatt boomed.

Jim stood up. "First, thank you all for your kindness. And thank you to my friend Marcus. Without him, I don't know if I could do any of whatever it is I do. I am sorry for letting you down. I am sorry I misused my gift, but I didn't know what else to do with it."

"Does anyone else have anything to say?" Wyatt asked.

"What did they do wrong?" the girl with purple hair asked as she rose from her seat. "What help did we give him? He's a real magician, unlike the rest of us. He doesn't deserve this. Marcus doesn't deserve this. This is wrong. It's wrong."

"Thank you, Ms. Starr. Does anyone else have anything to say?" Wyatt asked in a tone that was far from grateful for Dara's input.

"Ashamed! You should be ashamed of yourself," a voice near the front shouted. Jim looked in the direction of the shout, and saw Mel Hall looking at him through watery eyes filled with a combination of sorrow and anger. "I have spent my whole life hoping to find true magic. And you have it. But what did you do with it? You didn't advance the art or bring beauty to the world. You used it to cheat and rob. You have broken my heart. Shame on you! I want these two out of our Order. I want them to never darken these doors again. As far as I am concerned, they are dead to me, and to us all."

Jim trembled and the audience was silent.

Wyatt called for individual votes to expel Jim and Marcus. Both passed with Dara Starr casting the only dissenting vote in each case.

Wyatt summoned Jim and Marcus to the stage. "Please hand me your wands," he said when they reached him. The two did as instructed.

Wyatt snapped the wands in half. A tear streamed down Marcus' face, but his expression was otherwise stoic.

"Pursuant to the will of the Southern Magi, you James Lane, and you Marcus Wade, are hereby expelled from the Order of the Southern Magi and banned from these premises, effective immediately. Now go!"

Derrick led Jim, Marcus and Ally out of the auditorium. The audience was silent and angry. Dara mouthed "I'm sorry" at them as they passed. The group left the auditorium and Derrick led them straight to the door. As they walked out, they heard the lock bolt behind them. They walked up the stairs.

"Marcus, I'm sorry," Jim said.

"Don't. Let's not do this. Let's just say goodbye," Marcus said.

"How dare you," Ally started, but Jim interrupted her.

"Goodbye Marcus."

Marcus nodded and walked away, leaving Jim and Ally alone with the smell of barbecue pork hanging in the air.

***

The former members of the Mystic Order of the Broncos drifted apart after that. Whether it was a function of the incident or just a natural progression of time that tends to erode at old friendships, none of them would really be able to say.

Marcus' meeting in Los Angeles had been surprisingly productive. His manager got him a part on an episode of a television show. He played a magician who was accused of murder. In the end, it turned out the accusations were correct.

The producer liked him, and eventually got him his own show as the title character on *Harry Sherlock*, a dramedy about a magician who solves crimes. "Yes, it's been done before," Marcus would say. "But this time it's different. It has me, you see."

The show was moderately successful, and opened enough doors for Marcus that he continued to get parts here and there. It also helped boost his magic career, ultimately leading to a residency in a Vegas venue. That's where he met Peter, an executive with a record label. Marcus had no intention of getting into the music business, and Peter never tried to push him in that direction. In the end, Peter did offer a different kind of proposal, which Marcus accepted. Fifteen years had passed since the incident. None of the Broncos were invited to the wedding.

By all accounts, the marriage was solid and stable, and not just by show business standards. The Vegas residency ended after a long run, but the touring and acted continued. In interviews, Marcus always listed his marriage as his greatest accomplishment. Although he never said it, Marcus never really got over the night his wand and friendships were broken in that old building near the rib joint in Memphis.

Stan was eventually hired at an automotive supplier in Georgia. He met a girl. They married and had three kids. Stan was happy. He really didn't have any regrets.

Mel Hall died three months after Jim and Marcus were expelled from the Southern Magi.

Six years after that, Wyatt Taylor died of a heart attack. Nick had left the firm a couple of years before, and went solo. Eventually, he ran for and won a judicial seat in Oxford. He held that seat for the better part of a decade before the Governor, an old fraternity brother of his, nominated him to the Mississippi Supreme Court. He was confirmed and served with distinction until he retired.

Jim and Ally got married about a year after that night. They bought a nice house in a good area. Their casino winnings were enough for very healthy down payment plus a little more.

They settled into their jobs and their lives. Despite pressure from their families and society, they never had any children. They each worked their way up to comfortable enough mid-level management positions in their chosen fields.

Jim didn't use his powers. He and Ally thought that was for the best. Their life together was good. It was happy.

It just wasn't magical.

Twenty-Six Years Later

If the heat that May afternoon was any indication, it was going to be a horrible summer, even by Memphis standards. Memphis in May was usually warm with episodes of torrential rain. But this May was already hot and dry. Ally had suggested that by August, the whole city would feel like a sauna with the humidity cranked all the way up.

Jim had dozed off in his recliner, the book he was reading splayed open across his belly. Bronco, their yellow lab was asleep on the floor at his feet. Ally was in the front yard working on the small garden that had done nothing but frustrate her over the years, but she found that frustration to be somehow peaceful.

As Ally alternated between cursing and pruning, a bright metallic blue car came to a stop in front of their house. Ally stood up and watched as a woman in her late 30's or early 40's got out of the car. She was dressed in an outfit that tried to look casual, but which was impeccably professional. Her raven black hair had the same aesthetic.

"Ms. Lane?" the woman asked as she walked around the car.

"Yes," Ally said with a hint of suspicion.

The woman approached her with a smile.

"It's so good to meet you. Well, to see you again," the woman said extending her hand.

Ally instinctively reached out her hand. "I'm sorry, I'm not..."

The woman laughed. "You don't remember me. You wouldn't. I met you one time when I was a teenager. But it was a pretty memorable night. I'm Dara Starr. I saw your husband perform magic that night in '97. And, well, I was there the night he was asked to stop."

"Were you one of those..."

"Southern Magi, yes, I was," Dara said. "Still am. In fact, Ms. Lane, I'm kind of the head magi now."

"Oh?" Ally asked crossing her arms in front of her. "What can I help you with?"

"Can we get Mr. Lane? I owe him something."

"And what is that?" Ally asked.

"An apology to start."

Ally invited her in and roused Jim. Bronco showed some attention to the visitor, but resumed his nap after giving appropriate greetings and receiving the ear scratches he so richly deserved.

Dara reintroduced herself to Jim, and he remembered her after her explanation. "Mr. and Mrs. Lane, I am here with an apology and a request. Or an offer. I think you'll want to hear both."

"It's Ally and Jim," Ally said. "Let's have a seat. I have some tea in the fridge."

They sat around the kitchen table with sweaty glasses of tea. Ally explained that she owned a public relations firm in Midtown in addition to leading the Magi.

"I still do magic, of course," she said. "During college and for a while after, I did sleight of hand and illusions in clubs and with a couple of burlesque companies. I was good enough that the audience didn't care that I wasn't taking off any clothes, or at least they were nice enough to pretend they enjoyed it."

Dara drank from her glass. "I did, and still do, private parties. I'm not bad. Not as rock and roll as I used to be, but not bad."

"None of us are as rock and roll as we used to be," Ally said.

"You are right about that," Dara said smiling. "Long story short, I was given my golden wand maybe five years after I last saw you. Became the Magi's first female Magister a few years after that. I may be the longest serving Magister in the group's history, but I suspect Mel Hall holds that distinction. I'm sure you heard he passed away."

Jim said he had read that, as well as having read Wyatt Taylor's obituary.

"I'm happy for you, Dara," Jim said. "But..."

"Why am I here?" Dara asked. "The way the Order treated you has never sat well with me. I want to make amends."

"I appreciate that," Jim said. "But it's been a long time since all that happened."

"Yes. And I should have made contact years ago. I won't make excuses. I should have, but I didn't."

"No problem," Jim said.

"Jim, your gift is off the charts amazing," Dara said. "The Order had no business passing judgment on you. They sat on their high horse trying to look down on you, but you are so above all of them – all of us – that we would have strained our necks just trying to look up to you."

"Dara, that's very sweet," Ally said. "But we did kind of misuse Jim's...skill."

"Magic. He used his magic," Dara said. "And let's be clear. Those old men saw what you could do. They gave you no real guidance. They gave you a few rounds of applause and set you out into the world with no idea of how to use your magic. And when you used it in a way they didn't like they snapped your wand."

"And my friend's," Jim said.

"Marcus turned out fine," Dara said. "I'm worried about what we did to you. Jim, you are better than the rest of us because what you do is real. Which sets you apart from every member of the Magi, past, present, and future."

"I don't really do it anymore," Jim said. "Not in a long time."

"I know you don't perform, but you can still move objects, can't you?"

"I don't know," Jim said.

"What do you mean?" Dara asked.

"I haven't tried too much since back then," Jim said.

"Do you blame him?" Ally asked. "It caused him nothing but grief."

"I get that," Dara said. "But, I don't know, it's like owning an original Rembrandt and never looking at it because you associate it with a bad day."

"That's laying it on a bit thick," Ally said.

Dara laughed. "Fair. Jim, will you pass me some sweetener. The pink stuff," she said pointing at a caddy full of white and pink packets on the table.

Jim picked up one and handed it to her.

Dara put the packet down on the middle of the table.

"Pass it to me without touching it, okay?"

"He's not going to do that," Ally said. "He doesn't need to prove anything to you."

"I don't want him to prove anything to me," Dara said. "Prove it to yourself, Jim. I promise it's important."

Jim looked at Ally.

"Your call, babe. You sure don't need to prove anything to me," Ally said.

Jim sighed and faced Dara. He gestured and the packet trembled before inching across the table to her.

Dara smiled. "How did that feel?"

"It felt good," Jim said.

"I want you both to come to the Magi meeting next month. Can you do that?"

"I don't know," Jim said. "Why?"

"We need to give you a formal apology," Dara said. "It's time to re-hang the Rembrandt."

***

The building that housed the Southern Magi had not changed one bit in the intervening years. Dara met Jim and Ally at the door and ushered them into the meeting room, past the gathering members. The faces were not familiar. They were younger than the ones Jim and Ally had seen, and perceptibly, if not monumentally, less homogenous.

Dara asked them to sit in the front, which they did as the members filed in and put on their capes.

After welcoming the gathered members from the stage, Dara introduced a young woman who wordlessly performed a routine in which see seemingly made blue and red silks appear and disappear with movements almost perfectly timed to what could only be described as Eastern infused techno. It was well done and equally well received by the audience.

Dara then led the group through the tedious but necessary agenda items and announcements before turning her attention to Jim.

"We have with us a very special guest. Jim Lane was once a fellow Magi. Circumstances led to his departure. We can debate whether it was right or wrong to ask Jim to leave, but it is my sincere belief that the Southern Magi did Jim a great disservice," Dara said, looking at Jim with a warm smile.

"But, more importantly we deprived the Southern Magi and the world of magic of something truly special. To that end, Jim, will you join me up here, please."

Jim looked to Ally, who patted his hand. He stood up and walked towards the stage.

A small round of applause broke out as Jim took his place next to Dara.

"Jim, I am asking you if you are willing to share your

gift with us tonight. Will you?"

Jim looked out at the audience. Other than Ally, he did not recognize any audience members. He turned to Dara and said he would.

Dara turned her attention to a dull silver serving dish that looked like it had been purloined from a room service cart at an aging hotel. With a flourish, she grabbed the lid and flipped it dramatically. Underneath the lid was a plate with two green dice.

Dara put down the lid and scooped up the dice, twisting it in her hand to inspect them. "These are ordinary dice. No tricks. No magnets. Just dice. Does anyone want to confirm this?"

A young man in the front row walked up, handled and scrutinized the dice, confirming Dara's statement before sitting back down.

Dara placed the dice on the table.

"Jim, please show the Magi what magic really is."

Jim looked down and licked his lips. "I don't know if I can," he said softly to Dara.

"You can."

The entry door at the back of the meeting hall opened. Jim looked towards it and saw two men walking in. One of them was stylishly dressed with salt and pepper hair. It was Marcus.

Jim got caught in a stare looking at Marcus, who placed the tips of his fingers to his forehead and offered a hat-tipping gesture towards Jim. Ally looked back as well.

"Jim," Dara said. "You can do this."

Jim walked towards the table, and with a small gesture made one die rattle almost imperceptibly.

Ally smiled at Jim, and Marcus nodded.

Jim waved his hand again, creating another small tremor in the die. His throat was dry; his hands were shaking more visibly than the die. He could feel the audience growing restless in the room that was quiet except for the sounds of creaking chairs and a lone cough.

He looked up again and took a deep breath, and brought his arms to his chest.

"We have faith," Dara said.

"Love you, babe," Ally said from her seat.

"For the Mystic Order of the Broncos!" Marcus boomed from the back of the room, leading to scattered chuckles.

Jim smiled and closed his eyes. He flung his arms out from his chest. The dice rocketed off the table in opposite directions, clattering into the audience.

There was silence. Jim opened his eyes, waiting for the cascade of questions and doubt. But that's not what he got. The silence broke with a roar as the Magi shot to their feet cheering and shouting.

Jim's eyes teared up, as Ally rushed the stage and embraced him. Moments later, Marcus was beside them.

Dara turned to the Magi. "I will entertain a motion to reinstate Jim Lane and Marcus Wade to the Southern Magi."

"So moved," a dozen members shouted.

After receiving an enthusiastic second to the motion, Dara put it to a vote. By unanimous declaration Jim and Marcus's membership in the Southern Magi was reinstated following a quarter of a century ban.

Dara nodded to one of the other Magi, who brought her three narrow boxes. "I would also hear a motion to make Ally Lane an honorary Magi," Dara said. "She has earned it."

There was unanimous consent.

Dara handed Jim, Ally, and Marcus each a box. Inside were golden wands. "Welcome home," Dara said, as the assembled Magi burst into applause and cheers.

The three held each other, crying.

The Broncos – all of them – reconnected after that night, and made it a point to see each other as often as possible. Jim and Ally were regular attendees of Southern Magi meetings. They decided that Jim did not need to perform his magic publicly, and certainly did not need to use it again for questionable purposes. But what he did do was show it to magicians.

At first, it was just members of the Southern Magi. Over time, guest magicians would visit and marvel at Jim's abilities. Ally insisted, and Jim and Dara agreed, that anyone who saw watched Jim was required to swear that they would not discuss what they had seen outside of the magic community.

The magicians kept their oaths, but that certainly did not stop the word spreading within magic circles. As the years passed, hundreds of magicians made their way to the basement lair of the Southern Magi. Hundreds walked away impressed and even shaken.

Within a decade, Jim Lane's name was known and spoken with hushed reverence by practitioners around the world.

For the next thirty years, Jim and Ally were happy. Jim did not need a large audience, but he thrived on the small but knowledgeable ones that gathered to see him. Jim was given dozens of honorary titles by magic groups. But ultimately, it was his status as elder statesman with the Southern Magi that meant the most to him. He was given the office that once belonged to Mel Hall, which meant more to him than he could ever explain.

Jim Lane was 82 years old when he died, peacefully asleep next to Ally. The graveside service took place at Elmwood, a historic cemetery in Memphis. By the time Jim died, neither he nor Ally had any close biological family. But their chosen family was there.

Marcus, Stan, and Nick stood by Ally during the interment. The old friends were there for her and Jim and for each other. The surviving members of the Sorcerer's Table would spend the day laughing and crying after the funeral. Truth be told, the laughter was a bigger part of the day. And that meant the world to Ally.

Members of the Southern Magi decked out in their full regalia and other magicians who had met with Jim over the years attended the funeral. They were somber and quiet until the coffin was lowered into the ground, at which point they broke into a low, slow applause.

Jim's name and dates of life were etched into the white granite tombstone, along with a simple inscription.

True Magic.

After the mourners left, the grounds crew began their work. A younger man turned to his supervisor as he did his work.

"That was weird," the younger man said.

"You know, I've seen a lot of things out here over the years," the supervisor said. "But I got to say, I have never in my life seen so many capes."

The Flying Jaguar

Despite the intense cold and the circumstances, Michael Royal had to admit it was one hell of a view. Freezing wind whipped his face as he looked down at the white snow blanketed peak of the Finsteraarhorn, the highest of the numerous mountains in the Bernese Alps.

Michael flipped up the collar of his long, black wool coat to cover his ears and ran a hand through his copper red hair. The mountains were pretty to look at from above, but now was not the time to for sightseeing or waxing poetic on the beauty of geography. That was for later, or probably not at all.

Michael looked ahead and saw his target, a long, gray dirigible gliding through the air. Michael looked up at the white balloon carrying him, and pulled a lever on the control panel. Two metal canisters rose from the bottom of the gondola and extended from the side on iron tubes. Michael reached under his coat and pulled his Colt M1911A1 out of its brown leather holster. He cocked the weapon and slid the thumb safety off before placing the sidearm back into its holster. He looked through a pair of binoculars and made some quick calculations before pressing a red button. The canisters on the side of the gondola roared to life, shooting a stream of blue flames. Michael made small adjustments on two sticks, each causing one of the canisters to turn. The balloon carried Michael Royal towards the dirigible and an excellent chance at death.

***

You can pretend to be civilized all day and all night, but if you can't admit that there's a certain satisfaction in knocking out a guy's tooth with a well delivered punch, then you, my friend, are a liar.

The fight wasn't my fault. Honest.

I had been – more or less – minding my business, standing at the bar in the Thorn and Whistle, one of the more tolerable pubs in London. I had just ordered a pint when I overheard someone making a statement about how Britain would have won the war in time with or without "the Yanks." I looked at the man making the ridiculous statement. He was short and stubby, and built like a floor safe. Only uglier.

"You may want to reconsider that position, friend." I said.

He looked at me and managed to insult my American father, my Irish mother, and the good people of the United States all in one sentence in a thick Cockney accent. The insults about my parents were implied, admittedly, as the clown obviously didn't know exactly how my family tree branched, but he made some pretty good guesses by the leaves on display.

I retorted by pointing out that he should be a little more thankful, because it's all but impossible to speak German in a Cockney accent, and that he probably would not have risen in the ranks under a Nazi regime, what with him being far from the Uberman ideal.

His counter to this real reasoned line of rhetoric was to wheel around on me and throw a clumsy right hook, which I easily dodged. I then delivered a tight straight jab to his idiot mouth, which brings us back to where we started. I felt the tooth give way at the impact of my fist. I don't want to claim I'm some kind of Rocky Marciano, but I'm no palooka either. The truth is that the dope's tooth was already in bad shape, and I just helped it along. I did the guy a favor.

He doubled over and started coughing and sputtering until he finally managed to spit the tooth out.

Normally, you'd expect the man's buddies to get all sore and take it upon themselves to champion their pal by joining in the fray. The two guys the pug had been talking to, however, were too busy laughing at him to initiate a fight.

"I oughtta throw you out, but that guy is a horse's arse," said Karen Miller, the pub's proprietor and barkeep. "Besides, you pay your tab most of the time, so I'll let it slide. Here's your pint, slugger."

I sat on the stool that was covered in cracked black leather and happily drank. Regardless of my allegiance to the good old U.S. of A, you had to admit that the beer you get in the U.K. is superior to anything stateside. Fortunately, my business brought me to London on the regular.

"You really either need to make your fights less frequent or at least more exciting, Royal," said a familiar voice from behind me.

Without turning around, I said "Sorry to disappoint you, Baxter."

"I'll recover," Sir Kenneth Baxter said, sitting on the stool next to me. He was a tall, thin man in his late 50's with close cropped gray hair and a neatly trimmed mustache of the same color. "Thank you for making the trip."

"It's your dimes, Baxter," I said. He'd cabled a lot of dimes over to Boston. Sir Kenneth Baxter had a lot of money he was willing to dole out when he wanted something, which was often. Good for both of us that finding and obtaining things was basically my job description. Although the card simply said "Investigator". "Finding and obtaining things" was too wordy for a card, unless you made the letters so small you couldn't read them, which would defeat the entire purpose of the cards.

"There's a piece out there that I would like to procure," Baxter said.

"I assume it's not for sale?"

"It is. But I'd prefer not to pay the current owner as much as a single pound for it," Baxter said.

"Are you suggesting I steal something?"

"Liberate more than steal, Royal."

"You Brits tend to liberate a lot of art."

Baxter smiled. "Be that as it may, I assume your moral outrage, sincere though it may be, will be tempered when I tell you that the item in question is in the hands of Gunderschadt."

Henrich Gunderschadt, referred to himself as a Baron, despite no apparent right to the title. But, he had enough money that people went along with it. He had been relatively apolitical during the war and the years before, but he had been unerringly opportunistic. He had made a fortune brokering spoils of war, and, in the eight years since the war ended, he continued the business model.

Gunderschadt had fled Germany when he read the tea leaves, getting out while the getting was good. He had made his way to Switzerland and set up his business and life there.

I'd never met Gunderschadt personally, but, had crossed his wake a few times, and I'd seen him at an auction once. He was a tall, courtly man in his early 40's with blonde hair, and cold blue eyes. His mouth seemed to be perpetually curled into a slight sneer. He liked to wear an ornate uniform that made him appear to be part of a line of German royalty that didn't currently exist. The Baron carried an ivory handled sword in black leather scabbard on his left hip. By all accounts he could use the damn thing.

"Six weeks ago, a golden statue of a jaguar disappeared from a museum in Mexico City. Recently, word in certain circles spread that there will be an auction for the piece two weeks from today in Berne," Sir Baxter said.

"And you want me to get it before it gets to auction."

"I do indeed."

"I assume you don't want me to just return it to the museum."

"It will go to *a* museum, Royal. Albeit a different one."

I smiled, and shook my head. "Liberation."

"Quite. Now that your critique of British art curation is noted and, presumably, out of your system, my sources indicate that the piece is currently in Paris, but will be en route to his chalet in the Bernese Alps tomorrow."

"Train?" I asked.

"Dirigible. The Baron maintains a zeppelin, and it was spotted heading West near Berne yesterday. I assume it will pick up the jaguar and spirit it off to the Baron's compound until the auction."

"You want me to break into Gunderschadt's lair and nab the statue before the auction?"

"No. His compound is too secure. You wouldn't want to try that."

"Race to Paris and get the piece?"

"Too much security. It would raise quite the fuss. I think your best option is to intercept it between Paris and Gunderschadt's chateau."

"So, you want me to.... you can't be serious," I said.

"I am. But don't worry. I have a balloon you can use and can secure a private car on the Orient Express which leaves Paris tomorrow morning." Sir Baxter said. "It will be an adventure, Royal. Besides, you know I'm going to pay you so much to do this you can't decline."

He had a point.

"So, just to be clear, the plan is..."

"The plan is that you will ride the Arlberg-Orient-Express to Switzerland and launch the balloon from the roof of your car when you reach a designated location. It's marked on this map," Baxter said, handing Royal a map with a red circle around a location in Switzerland, west of Zurich.

"And then . . ." Royal said.

"And then you catch the dirigible. It's obvious, really," Baxter said. "Don't worry, we've got rockets on the balloon."

"Sounds safe," Royal said.

"Oh, God no," Baxter said. "I wouldn't have to pay you so much money if it was remotely safe."

***

There were a dozen wooden crates in the hold, all stamped with a symbol of a large bird surrounded by flames. Getting from the balloon Baxter provided and onto the Baron's zeppelin was not easy, but Royal accomplished it with the help of a grappling hook fired from a special cannon, some rope, and his U.S. Army issued knife. It was unlikely Royal had successfully snuck onboard. Someone surely saw the air balloon shoot towards the zeppelin. And even if not, the odds that it wouldn't be noticed lashed to the side were small since the set up was causing the whole shebang to list to port.

Royal's time aboard the vessel was going to have to be short.

Royal slammed the end of a crowbar under the lid of the crate nearest him and cracked the top open. He found some stone carvings inside, but no jaguar. Michael pried open the next container. Inside, covered by layers of straw, he found the statue. It was a two-foot long depiction of a jaguar pouncing as if it were taking down prey. It was solid gold with sections painted enamel black, though many of those areas were faded or scratched. Michael admired the jaguar briefly before sticking into the khaki cloth bag he had slung over his shoulder.

That was too easy, Royal thought. As if on cue, he heard a door fly open and saw two men climbing down the metal stairs into the zeppelin's hold. The stairs, of course, were between him and the hole in the side of the vessel through which Royal had entered.

The first man down the stairs was large and muscular, dressed in black pants and a black sweater. He was carrying a long wooden staff. Behind him was a man dressed in an immaculate military style uniform, with a sword on his side.

Royal stood up, and pushed back his coat to draw the Colt from its holster. "Stand back, Gunderschadt. I'm just taking the jaguar. You can keep the rest of your stolen baubles."

The Baron put a hand on the shoulder of his associate. "Hold on, Auguste." The man with him stopped and fixed a homicidal glare on Royal. They stood about ten feet from each other on the narrow metal walkway between the platform where the stairs came down from the main quarters of the zeppelin to the wider, metal grid floor where the crates and Michael Royal stood. The walkway was not wide enough for two men to walk side by side, especially if one of them was as large as Auguste.

"You two back up," Royal ordered, levelling the Colt at the larger man's chest.

"Before you fire that weapon, we need to discuss a few things," the Baron said.

"What's that?"

"First, allow us some pleasantries. I am Baron Heinrich Gunderschadt, and this is my associate, Auguste Maes. He is Belgian, and I am, for the time being, Swiss. Might you be so kind as to tell us who you are?"

"Michael Royal. American, and part of the reason you are currently 'Swiss.' I won't be taking advantage of your hospitality for long. So, please go back up the stairs so I can get out of here. Or this zeppelin won't be the only thing with holes in it."

"As to that, Mr. Royal," the Baron said, "I must advise you that firing that gun may be problematic."

Royal cocked his head to one side, keeping his finger on the trigger of his semi-automatic.

"Hydrogen, Mr. Royal. One misplaced spark and we go up in a ball of fire. You, me, poor Auguste, plunge into the mountains in a spectacular blaze."

"Kind of like a phoenix," Michael said, lowering his gun slightly.

The Baron smiled at that. "Not really, Mr. Royal. I am afraid nothing would arise from our ashes. Now, put down the gun so we can limit the casualties in the regrettable business to follow."

Michael holstered his Colt and pulled out his knife as Auguste barreled towards him. The Belgian swung the staff with savage force, missing Royal's head by inches, striking a metal support. Michael scrambled backwards as Auguste raised the staff again, swinging it at Royal's head. Michael avoided a crushed skull, but the staff smashed into his left shoulder with an audible crack that sent bolts of pain shooting through his arm. Michael staggered backwards.

The Belgian charged, and Michael twisted to one side, slamming his fist into the back of Auguste's head, disorienting and sending him careening into a crate. Royal arced his knife across the Belgian's right arm, slicing his sweater and drawing a thick line of red blood. Auguste spun, swinging the staff. Michael ducked but lost his footing and fell. Auguste smiled, raising the staff for what could have been a death blow. As he swung, Michael, his back against a crate, leveraged all his strength to kick Auguste's legs out from under him. The Belgian fell violently, careening into a crate and off the platform. The outer shell of the zeppelin caught him, sagging only slightly.

As Auguste struggled to get to his feet, Baron Gunderschadt withdrew the sword from its scabbard. Light from the hole in the side of the zeppelin gleamed off the blade.

With a sneer, the Baron approached deftly flicking the blade. Michael clamored to his feet and faced Gunderschadt. His left arm was screaming in pain. He held his knife in his right.

The Baron advanced, thrusting the sword at Royal. Michael spun out of the way as the blade sliced his wool coat. The Baron swung the sword with wicked precision that would have bit into Royals head had he not dropped to the ground at the exact right moment. Michael rolled to his left and dropped his knife, picking up the lid of an open crate. No sooner had he picked it up than the Baron was on top of him, executing a lunge for Royal's throat. Michael held up the lid like a shield. The blade drove into and through it, stopping a hair's breadth from Royal's Adam's apple.

The Baron attempted to pull the blade back, but it was stuck in the lid. Michael wrenched the wooden crate lid with all his strength, causing his left shoulder to erupt in pain. But the effort was worthwhile, as he tore the sword from the Baron. Michael flung the lid and the sword over the edge of the platform and grabbed his knife. Gunderschadt backed away from him, allowing Royal to move closer to his escape route.

"Mr. Royal, you are making a monumental error. Leave the Jaguar and we will call this even."

"I make a lot of errors, Herr Baron. It's what I do. Now, why don't you goosestep back up those stairs while I leave and no one has to get hurt. At least not any worse."

The Baron grinned. "As you wish, Mr. Royal," he said as he turned and began to slowly ascend the stairs.

Michael ran toward the hole, but just as he reached it, he felt a tug on his coat, stopping him short. Michael fell, and Auguste was on him. The Belgian smashed his fist into Royal's injured shoulder, causing the American to scream. The Belgian grabbed Michael and lifted him to his feet, spinning him around.

"Mr. Royal, have a safe return flight. Auguste, take back what is mine and then show him out," the Baron said from the top of the stairs. "Auf Widersehen, Mr. Royal."

Auguste reached into Michael's bag and recovered the jaguar. He grinned, and then pushed Michael out of the zeppelin.

Royal tumbled before grabbing a rope that held the balloon to the side of the zeppelin. He dropped his knife and it fell silently into space towards the mountain peaks. Michael scrabbled with his feet on the side of the zeppelin, his arms shrieking in pain as he pulled on the rope. By sheer force of will, he pulled his way up to the gondola. As Michael hauled himself into the balloon's basket, Auguste leaned from the zeppelin, grabbing the collar of Michael's jacket. The zeppelin again lurched, causing Auguste to stumble. Michael slammed his entire weight backwards, pulling Auguste out of the opening. The jaguar fell from his hands and bounced by Royal, who was almost able to grab it. Almost.

The Belgian's arms flailed wildly as he shot past the gondola and into the bright, blue sky. He almost looked like he could fly. He could not, and neither could the jaguar, which glinted in the sun as it tumbled and dove out of sight.

Michael turned the burners on, inflating the balloon, and then disengaged the hook from its cannon freeing the rope. The balloon drifted away from the zeppelin as the Baron stood in the hole, looking out at him. Michael raised the Colt towards him, and the Baron clicked his heels together and nodded at Royal before turning away.

Michael lowered his weapon and slumped into the gondola. He peered over the edge and looked down at the mountains below him.

Michael Royal laughed as it occurred to him that there probably aren't any museums on top of the Finsteraarhorn.

Random Lines From That Cybertech Thriller I Am Writing

I am going through the final edits for my new cybertech thriller, "*Halcyon 7: The Halifax Collective Chronicles, Volume 1.*" I hope these lines breakthrough your firewalls of resistance, and lead you to buy a copy from your favorite virtual or brick and mortar bookseller.

1. "Don't give me that 'White Hat/Black Hat' nonsense, Linus," growled Gabriel. "All our hats are grey and you damn well know it."

2. "The fact that you even know about Bitcoin means it's deader than Schrodinger's Cat probably is," said Natal33 with a smirk.

3. The Halcyon7 Wyrm was attacking the firewall with a speed that no one could have anticipated, including the elite security team for DataMax Corp.

4. "A healthy diet of Onions and VPN will make you live a lot longer," Gabriel said. "It's better than exercise and a gluten-free diet for my money."

5. "The greatest hack of all is simply to let them underestimate you. And they always do," Natal33 said as she finished off another can of CaffeinePure Blue.

6. "Our customers think they merely use our products. The fact, ladies and gentlemen, is that our users are our product. The utility they gain from our software is merely ornamental," Chairman Dazuki told the DataMax board members who nodded in agreement.

7. Linus adjusted the control of the VR rig and leaned back. He had earned some time to relax. By morning, he would be dead.

8. The lights of Tokyo cast long shadows.

9. Within milliseconds Natal33 had stolen the identities of all of DataMax Corp.'s 8321 employees, but only one of them mattered. And she got it. Chairman Dazuki was hers. Or rather she was now him in every way that mattered.

10. "A third grader could have spotted that hole in the defenses. And I skipped third through fifth grades."

11. "Morality is a luxury we can't afford," Gabriel said. "The Corporations certainly can afford that luxury, but they don't avail themselves of it as it conflicts with maximizing shareholder value."

12. "God is not in the code," Natal33 said. "God is the code."

Christmas at Sir Percival's Estate

11- October-1977

My manservant Hudson woke me today with a platter of eggs and toast corners. He affected a Scottish brogue and proclaimed that he was captain of a loch vessel. Every day he is full of such nonsense! I never know what he will claim to be on any given day. But I know that one thing shall always remain constant. Hudson is loyal to fault, even when he is nowhere to be found.

13-October-1977

It has arrived! Hudson, who today claims to be a French ballooning magnate Viscount Pierre du Pekingese, informed me that the new piano arrived! Ah! I look forward to playing it night after night alone in the very front of my manor! What a delight this shall be!

20-October-1977

Someone has bought Lord Bunkley's property on the land next to mine. I saw them from a distance today. It seemed like a lovely family. I shall have Hudson invite them over for a proper tea. Perhaps I will play piano for them!

23-October-1977

The new lord of the Bunkley manor visited today. He is a gentleman named Bowie, and is apparently a musician of some sort. He thanked me for the invitation, which Hudson delivered in the guise of a prawn merchant from Brussels named Adelhard Eikenboom. Following a cup of tea and a discussion of our business interests, I showed Mr. Bowie my piano and played for him. He thanked me and asked if he could come back and "borrow" the piano sometime. I asked him if he could not afford his own piano, and he just silently gazed at his feet dejectedly. I felt bad for the gentleman and advised him he was welcome to play it. He seemed to feel better.

24-October-1977

Mr. Bowie showed up at my door unannounced and demanded to play my piano. I informed him that I was planning on using it, and he reminded me that I told him he could play. As a gentleman, I was obliged to let him play. Which he did for six hours. While he does have some skill, it was an appalling intrusion. Hudson pretended to be a big game hunter named Mountechuck the entire time.

25-October-1977

Bowie returned! He once again requested to play my piano. I advised him I had looked him up, and saw no reason why he could not purchase his own piano, as he appears to have had enormous sales with some song about the cartoon character Ziggy, and was himself a Duke of some sort. Mr. Bowie just shook his head and gazed into space, saying "I can't afford a piano. I . . . I just can't."

I felt sorry for the lad and informed him that he could use the piano from time to time, but only if I am not present. I informed him that if I am around and he tries to use the piano, I will never let him play it again. He thanked me profusely, on the verge of tears, telling me I would never regret my decision.

12-November -1977

I have returned from a 4-day business trip to France. Hudson (who now calls himself Ursula Wishbone) informed me that Mr. Bowie came around every night during my absence, sheepishly asking if I was around and playing piano until the early dawn hours. He is an oddity, this Bowie. I would buy him a piano myself, but that feels inappropriate. He has, thus far, stuck to our agreement, and he does no harm in my absence.

I can think of no excuse to end the arrangement.

30-November-1977

I received correspondence from my third cousin twice removed from America, who is not as affluent as am I. His name, unlikely though it may be, is Bing. He is apparently a "crooner," which I am told is a singer of some sort. For reasons that elude me, he has requested to spend the holidays at my home. I told him I would be in Zurich during that time, yet he insisted that I allow him to come nonetheless. I asked if he planned to bring his family, and he informed me that he preferred to spend the holidays alone wandering around a giant empty house. I do not know why musicians are drawn to my home, but there you are. Hudson will have to keep an eye on the situation. Cousin Bing said he would arrive shortly.

4-December-1977

Bing's cab arrived at the house shortly after 6. I walked out to greet him, and saw Mr. Bowie lurking behind a bush. He caught sight of me and immediately scampered away like a frightened ocelot. I am heading off to Switzerland tomorrow, so I spent a brief dinner with Bing and wished him a Merry Christmas. I warned him about Mr. Bowie.

20-December-1977

Hudson has informed me that Mr. Bowie has visited nightly since my departure. He and cousin Bing have been awkwardly singing Christmas carols at night. Hudson informed me that it is oddly charming.

26-December-1977

I have spoken to Hudson, who is now pretending to be a geisha named Doris. He informed me that Cousin Bing and Mr. Bowie have started to quarrel. It seems Mr. Bowie insists on coming by and singing *The Little Drummer Boy* every night. Cousin Bing has stated that he would like to be left alone for a bit, and further protested that Christmas had passed. Mr. Bowie loudly reminded Cousin Bing that he is allowed to use the piano anytime that I am not around, and that Cousin Bing has no say in the matter. Bing relented, but would only half-heartedly pa-rump-pa-pa-pum before the awkward night ended.

29-December-1977

News is grim. Hudson informs me that Cousin Bing has become enraged to the point of swinging a golf club at Mr. Bowie, who loudly and repeatedly screams "Peace on Earth! Can it be!" after each swing. Following two full hours of this, Bing began to swing wildly at my precious piano! Hudson, who was hiding behind a settee pretending to be a container of liniment, reported that with each blow Bowie became more and more despondent. Finally, after Bing grew tired of swinging the club, the piano lay in ruins! Mr. Bowie reportedly sat amongst the debris wailing, "Where shall I ever find a piano I can use again!" and "Do you know what pianos cost? I cannot afford one, can you Bing? Can you?" In the morning, Bing left the house in a huff, saying nary a word to either Hudson or Bowie, who remained prostrate on the ruined piano until the following evening.

I return home tomorrow.

1-January-1978

I have dispatched correspondence to Cousin Bing and Mr. Bowie. Neither of them is allowed on my property again. The piano is beyond repair, and I had Hudson haul the ruins away. He did so while pretending to be an imp called Mr. Jellybones. I shall not replace the piano. Perhaps I will fill the space with statues or uncomfortable furnishings. In any event, there shall never be another musician in my home.

15-January-1978

Mr. Bowie has sold the Bunkley Estate. I saw him gazing longingly towards my home as he was driven away. I still do not know why the man cannot simply buy a piano to call his own.

3-February-1978

Hudson has started standing by my bed in a green grocer's costume singing "pa-rump-pa-pa-pum" at me as I sleep. I fear this nightmare shall never end.

Tower of the Necromancer

Nisra's crossbow bolt pierced the pigman's skull, killing it in an instant. Had she missed, the beast would have buried its battle ax into the back of her companion. Bardok pulled his sword out of the belly of another pigman and spun to face the one Nisra had dispatched.

"Nice shot," he said.

"Of course it was," Nisra responded, slinging the small crossbow over her shoulder.

Six pigmen lay dead. Bardok had a minor cut on his left bicep, but otherwise they had no injuries.

"I'll loot them," Nisra said.

"There is no time for that," a grave voice said from behind her.

"I swear if you don't stop appearing behind people, you're going to end up with a dagger in your belly," Nisra said.

"Doubtful," an old man replied, as he walked past her. The wizard reached into a bag cinched to the simple belt holding together his brown robes. He pulled out a small crystal and squeezed it in his left hand. "We are losing ground. We must go. Now."

Bardok sheathed his sword and nodded. "Your coin, your rules. Lead the way." Nisra considered protesting, but thought better of it.

Three nights earlier, the wizard spied Bardok and Nisra in the Dagger and Scroll tavern in the town of Journeys Far. The inn was full of reprobates and dirt. And dirty reprobates. Bardok was well into his cups, and the cups of anyone else who would part with theirs, and was regaling all who would listen with tales of his latest adventures.

Bardok was tall and broad-chested. His dark arms bore the red markings of the Sungara warriors, known for their skill with a blade and their strength. He was a foot taller than most men in the room. Two feet more than some.

"We were surrounded on all sides by spiders larger than apes. There were also some apes," Bardok said.

"There were no apes," Nisra said, sitting at a table. She wore a mossy green cloak covering her slightly pointed ears, but her dark complexion, thin, arched eyebrows and jet black eyes announced to the world that she was an elf from the southern lands.

"But the spiders . . ." Bardok continued.

"Oh yes. Those were there. And they were horrifyingly large. This part is true. Maybe not as big as an ape, but big enough. Do go on."

"I faced the foul beasts and my sword spoke loudly for me. I cleaved one then the other, drenching the forest floor with their devilish blue blood. Before I was done, ten of them lay dead by my hand."

"In fairness, half were dead by mine, but why quibble?" Nisra said, taking a drink from her tankard of ale.

"Those spiders will not do harm to travelers in the Darknight Woods. And they will not feast on the good people of Journeys Far, thanks to me!"

"Us," Nisra said with a smile.

The crowd applauded and offered thanks. They conspicuously did not offer any coins. As the tavern's patrons dispersed, Bardok sat next to Nisra.

"These people are holding onto their purses as if they thought we were going to rob them," Bardok said.

"Is that an option?" Nisra asked.

"You know what happened last time," Bardok said with a frown.

"The dungeons of Narimoor are unpleasant. Very drafty." Nisra said. "Fine. But you must improve your story telling ability, Bardok. We will starve if we have to rely on your charm."

As they commiserated, Levin approached them. He carried a plain wooden staff in his right hand.

"Might I buy you two slayers of spiders a drink?" he asked.

"I won't say no, wizard," Bardok said.

"Now, what makes you say I'm a wizard," Levin said, a twinkle in his pale blue eyes.

"The beard," Bardok said.

"Also, the stick," Nisra added. "Dead giveaway that."

Levin laughed. "May I join you?"

"If you make good on that drink, you can," Nisra said.

Levin waved to the barkeep, holding up three fingers. "You are both far from home," he said as he sat.

"One's home is not a prison, wizard."

"Profound," the wizard said nodding. "My name is Levin. My home is in the Malicorn Hills, one day from here."

"Never been there, Levin," the warrior said. "I am Bardok, and this is Nisra."

"Pleasure," Nisra said.

The barkeep, a squat barrel of a man, arrived and plunked three wooden tankards on the table. Levin handed him some cooper pieces from the purse dangling from his rope belt.

"Thank you for the drink," Bardok said. "To your health!"

Bardok drained his tankard in a heartbeat before gifting the table with an enormous belch.

"He's rude," Nisra said. "But in fairness, he's also smelly."

"Better to be alive and smelly than dead and smelling of a field of flowers!" Bardok said.

"Doesn't really work like that, Bardok," Nisra said.

"Well, as long as he is as good with a sword as he claims to be, manners are not a major concern," Levin said.

"No manners are equal to my blade," Bardok said, bursting into hearty laughter.

"I do not get your joke," Levin said, pulling a pipe from his belt pouch.

"He doesn't either, but it's funny to him and that's what matters, yes?" Nisra said

"In any event, wizard, we have enjoyed your generosity. But, I wager that you want more than a drink and Bardok's wit."

"A fool's wager it would be on my part," Levin said with a grin. He packed some tobacco into the pipe. He held the bowl of the pipe, which was a white carving of a dragon. He placed the stem in his mouth, and the bowl began to change from white to brown, as smoke began to form on the top of the tobacco. Levin took a puff and blew a ring towards the tavern's low ceiling.

"How did you light your pipe?" Bardok asked, his head tilted to the side like a curious pup.

"Magic. It is what I do," Levin said. "I need your help to stop another who also uses magic, but for purposes far more dire than heating some tobacco."

"Is that right?" Bardok asked.

"It is. Now, let me tell you a story," Levin said, blowing a ring of smoke that hovered above them before coalescing into a blueish white ball that pulsed and then exploded, enveloping the three of them in a curtain of smoke.

***

She was striking, this girl. She appeared to be twenty-five years old with long red hair and green eyes. She wore a simple black outfit with a dark burgundy hooded cape that accentuated her pale skin. She stood quietly with a thin smile. Her black horse neighed behind her where it had been tethered to a post.

Levin looked at her as she stood in the doorway of his home, then once again read the scroll she had given him. The girl said her name was Mara, and that she had travelled to the Malicorn Hills from the town of Gentry, a fortnight's journey from Levin's home. The scroll was a letter of introduction from Jartan, an old friend of Levin's. Jartan was no wizard, but he was a practitioner of magic. Levin's skills eclipsed his three-hundred-fold.

Jartan had sent Mara to Levin for training. Levin's friend explained that the girl had talent that exceeded Jartan's abilities to cultivate.

Levin sighed. He had neither the time nor the interest in mentoring anyone. But, Jartan was an old friend, and he could tolerate babysitting for a week, perhaps. He doubted the girl had potential. Mainly because he'd never met anyone who really did.

Levin dropped the parchment on a table and stepped out of the doorway. He turned his back on the girl. "We begin in the morning. Your room is there," he said pointing the red gemmed top of his staff towards a closed wooden doorway.

Mara surprised Levin by being awake before him the next morning. When he walked out of his bed chamber, he found her fully dressed for the day, sitting at the wooden dining table with various vials and jars in front of her.

"These are mine," she said by way of greeting. I would not presume to use anything of yours until you tell me to."

"I see. And what are you doing?"

"I am making potions. This one is quite nice," she said holding up a vial with a cloudy cerulean liquid.

Levin raised an eyebrow. "Healing, is it?"

She smiled.

Levin nodded. He could tell by sight that she had made it correctly. Not grand sorcery, but certainly it showed she did have talent and knowledge already.

"Do you want to try it?" she asked.

"First I must make a potion of clarity," Levin said.

"I am not familiar with that," Mara said.

"Some simply call it coffee," Levin said, waving his staff near a tin pot that started to glow.

After breakfast, Levin gauged Mara's skills. She could make minor potions and could read magical writing. More importantly she understood the natural flow of magic and had a rudimentary grasp of how to shape it. Levin worked with her and helped her learn how to harness that flow. From time to time she showed true ability, but would quickly lose control over the spells the old wizard taught her. After five days of training, Levin knew his old friend Jartan was right to send the girl to him.

When they were not training, Levin would ask her questions about her past and about Jartan. She was reluctant to discuss her personal history, providing only vague details, refusing to say much about her family. She spoke fondly of Jartan, saying she had been guided to him by a family friend. Jartan had helped her with potions, but his abilities did not extend much beyond that.

One evening, about a week into her training, Mara asked Levin about his staff.

"I know the gemstone is the key to the power, is it not?" she asked.

"Yes and no," Levin said. "When a wizard is ready he – or she – finds the right stone to craft their staff. Or wand. Or scepter. The form does not matter much."

"Why a staff then?" Mara asked.

"I find it helps me focus energy. It also helps me walk, as I am damnably old," Levin said with grin.

Mara laughed. Something about that laugh caught Levin off guard. It seemed to have a cold edge. It was probably nothing, Levin thought, but it worried at him. Mara seemed to notice, and she stopped. They sat in silence for a brief time.

"So, you use the gemstone in your staff to channel power?" she said

"That is correct. Channels and amplifies."

"How do you find the gem. That is enormous," Mara said, looking at the red stone in Levin's staff.

"It is late. We can discuss gemstones another day. Tomorrow, we will work on bending energy."

"Of course," Mara said, lowering her eyes.

Levin stood and walked towards his room.

"Thank you," Mara said.

"For what?" Levin asked.

"Teaching me. I feel I could learn much from you," she said with a smile that said more than her words. "I could learn so much."

Levin looked at her. "Good night, Mara. We will learn more in the morning."

As the days passed. Mara did learn. She was becoming more confident in her abilities and more adept at using them. Levin had never had a pupil develop so quickly. He did not forget the night they had spoken of gemstones and of Mara's unspoken offer, but for the next two weeks, Levin did not find any further reason for concern.

"Let's discuss gemstones," Levin said one morning.

Gemstones, he explained, are what elevate a conjurer into a wizard. Once one can find and craft a stone, they are no longer a student.

"The stones amplify a wizard's ability to control energy. It is what makes a wizard both great and potentially terrifying."

"How so?"

"With the right knowledge and a proper stone, a wizard can conjure fire from thin air, can control the minds of men, some have even been known to animate armies of the dead."

"Necromancy," Mara said.

"Indeed. That and more," Levin said.

"How do you find a stone?" Mara asked.

"It is hard to explain, but when you are ready, you simply go looking for it and you will find it."

"And how long does that take?" Mara asked.

"It varies. Some never do. The lucky ones find them after a decade of study."

"Ten years!" Mara said.

"So they say," Levin said. "Personally, I've never met anyone, myself included, who found their gem in less than fifteen."

"Can I not just buy one?"

"I suppose it is possible, but unlikely. No wizard will sell their stone. It would diminish their power significantly."

"What happens to stones of wizards when they die?" she asked.

"The stone fades with them."

Mara nodded, perhaps knowingly, Levin thought. "What if someone steals a stone?" she asked.

"Now, that is a very good question," Levin said, pulling a golden necklace out from under his shirt. The necklace held a small red stone pendant that matched the large red gem on his staff. "This is a control stone. When a wizard crafts his stone, a small piece is retained. The energy of the larger and small piece fuse. In short, a wizard can use the small piece to locate its big brother. And, in a dire situation, the wizard could simply destroy the small piece."

"What would that do?" Mara asked.

"It would destroy the stone and all magic it had created."

"What if one obtained a wizard's large and small stones?"

"That would be, shall we say, a problem. The stones would transfer to the one who took them, assuming they could harness energy in the first place."

"And if the original wizard were to die then? Would the stone be destroyed?" Mara asked.

"Once the stones take on a new home, the fate of the original owner becomes, irrelevant," Levin said. "But, that is hypothetical, of course. No wizard would let that happen. Most would not even let anyone know where the small stone is kept."

"I see," Mara said.

"Now, let's get to work for today, yes?" Levin said, and he and Mara worked the remainder of the day.

That evening, Mara prepared a special meal for them, saying it was an old family recipe. When Levin asked what the occasion was, Mara said he was owed a thank you for his patience and assistance on the path to magic.

The meal, including a spiced goat stew, was delicious. After clearing the bowls, Mara poured wine, saying it was a special bottle she had brought with her.

Levin took his goblet and raised it to Mara in a toast.

"May this day prove us all worthy of magic!"

And he took a drink. Moments later, his limbs stiffened, and he was unable to move.

"One of us surely is, dear Levin," Mara said, standing up. She walked behind her mentor, placing her hands on his shoulders.

"I'm afraid the poison is quite potent and unavoidably deadly, Levin. And honestly, I thought you would not be as easy a mark as that fool friend of yours, Jartan."

Levin tried to speak, but was not able to do so.

"He is quite dead, alas. Perhaps you will meet him soon. But do not worry, death is only a beginning. Maybe I will bring you back to serve in my army, yes?"

Mara leaned close to Levin's ear. "I am quite the necromancer, you know. You old men are so easy to fool. A pretty face and even the smallest pretense of helplessness is all that is needed to pry anything at all from your type."

She kissed Levin's cheek and reached inside his shirt, lifting his necklace over his head.

"You were so kind to show me this pendant, Levin. It kept me from weeks if not months of pretending to be a babe lost in the woods."

She slipped the necklace over her head and picked up Levin's staff. She walked back to the other side of the table.

"It looks good on me, don't you think?"

Levin sat unable to speak. His eyes looked at her, not with anger, but with disappointment.

"This is where we, or at least I, say goodbye, Levin," Mara said. "The potion will wear off eventually, but unfortunately it will be after you have died. That will take a few days, I am afraid. But, please believe me. This is not personal. You were certainly kinder than most wizards I have encountered. Alas, this is how things must be. Farewell, Levin."

Mara turned and walked out of the home, not pausing to pick up her belongings and not looking back.

***

"But, as you can see, I am quite alive," Levin said.

"Would have been quite the twist to the tale were you not," Nisra said.

"But the poison, why did it not kill you?" Bardok asked.

"I knew it was coming and I was prepared for it. I took a potion beforehand that I knew would counteract whatever she threw at me," Levin said.

"Why, though?" asked Nisra. "If you knew Mara was going to betray you, why did you not just take a more direct route to dealing with her?

"I had to be sure," Levin said, relighting his pipe. "I wanted to know how dangerous she really was. And what she said confirmed she is quite dangerous indeed."

"You let this witch steal your staff and the control stone. Surely that will just make her even more powerful. Sounds to me like whatever your plan was, it was foolish," Bardok said, motioning for another serving of ale.

"Indeed," said Levin. "Letting her get my control stone would have been a disastrous failure. Fortunately, that did not happen."

Levin opened his hand to reveal a small red stone on a golden chain. "I am many things, but a fool is not one of them. I showed her a fake, and that is what she stole."

"Nicely done," Nisra said.

Levin nodded. "It took a day for the potion to wear off even with my precautions. I have followed the stone since, and know she came through this charming town in the past day or two. I am close."

"And why are you telling us all this, wizard?" Bardok asked.

"I need assistance. Suffice to say that if this necromancer reaches her full power, she will unleash a blight of evil throughout the land."

"So, you are appealing to our better nature to help you?" Nisra asked.

"Heavens no. I have gold, and lots of it," Levin said seeming to produce a pouch out of thin air. He tossed it onto the table. "I think this should be sufficient to pique your interest."

Bardok picked up the bag, weighing it in his hand. "You have our interest. And our weapons. What now?"

"Now we save the world. Or at least my staff," Levin said.

***

Levin squeezed the red crystal tight in his right palm as he looked past the corpses of the pigmen. "She is an hour away if we move quickly."

"Bardok, let's find the horses. The creatures spooked them pretty badly," Nisra said.

Levin waved a hand and whistled a short tune. "There is no need to look," he said, as their three horses walked calmly from the woods to them.

Nearly an hour later, Nisra spotted a black riderless horse grazing by the side of the path. The elf looked to Levin, who nodded, indicating it was Mara's horse. Nisra dismounted and readied her crossbow in a fluid motion. Mara's horse bolted, running off the path and into the woods.

Before Bardok and Levin could get off their horses, Nisra was in pursuit, her green cloak fluttering behind her. She did not get far into the woods before she was stopped short by the sight of what looked like a black doorway floating just above the ground, surrounded by a shimmering blue light.

"She figured out how to create a portal," Levin said from behind Nisra's shoulder.

"If I had a dagger out, Levin," Nisra started.

"But you do not," Levin interrupted.

"What is that thing," Bardok said, running up to the other two.

"It is the way to Mara," Levin said. "Come."

Levin walked into the doorway and vanished.

"We aren't following him, are we?" Nisra asked.

"Why not? Adventure awaits!"

Nisra arched an eyebrow at him.

"There's also the rest of the money to consider," Bardok said with a grin. He bumped Nisra's shoulder with his. "Let's go."

Nisra sighed. "After you."

***

They walked through the portal and instantly came out on the other side. A small tingle traced its way down their spines, but otherwise the passage itself was unremarkable. What they found on the other side was a different story.

On this side, the portal looked like a large mirror surrounded by a halo of blue light. The glowing mirror was the most normal thing they could see. In front of them was a looming tower with no walls, made of what appeared to be metal beams. The tower reached 200 feet into the gray daytime sky. Between the mirror and the tower, the ground was strewn with the bodies of men, most of whom were wearing white helmets, but no other armor. They seemed to be wearing common cloth garments, but not like any Bardok and Nisra had seen before.

A sign with odd, red characters "Caution! Watch For Falling Materials!" was posted in the ground.

The area around the tower was surrounded by a metal fence, and large yellow metal constructs were scattered about.

"Listen to me!" Levin said. "We do not have time to gawk. It seems that Mara has slain the tower's guardians."

"But," he added pointing at the yellow constructs, "be

aware! There are golems that may take up the mantle!"

"Maybe worry more about the necromancer!" Nisra said, pointing to a red robed figure scaling the tower like a spider.

"Mara!" shouted Levin in a booming voice. "You shall stop!"

Even from the ground they could hear her cold laugh. She turned to face them and waved the staff with a glowing red crystal on the top, and then she continued to skitter up the tower.

The sky turned pale red, and the group felt a shudder on the ground. The corpses of the white-helmeted guards began to twitch.

"Prepare to fight!" Levin shouted at Nisra and Bardok as he dashed towards the tower.

Bardok drew his sword and Nisra pulled a rod from her belt. She flicked it, and it telescoped into a metal staff.

Two dozen corpses stood at the same time and shambled towards them.

Bardok and Nisra stood back to back.

"Adventure, indeed," Nisra said.

***

Mara reached the top of the tower. She surveyed the strange land, filled with towers and steel beasts moving along the roadways. She smiled. This would do nicely. She pointed the staff towards the ground and a scarlet bolt forked and struck the constructs on the ground.

"Hello, Levin," she said, not looking behind her. "Do we talk or fight?"

***

Nisra spun the rod, slamming it into the heads of the animated guards. Bardok swung his sword, cutting others down. The animated dead warriors had lost in skill they may have had in life, and attacked with mindless brute force. Some wielded metal tools at them, but most just tried to grasp and bite them. The fight was not difficult, but served Mara's purpose of delaying her pursuers.

As the last guard fell, Nisra and Bardok ran towards the tower. They covered half the distance when a scarlet bolt struck the constructs. The metal creatures roared to life and moved to block the adventurer's progress. One had what looked like a large metal plow that raised and slammed into the ground in front of them.

"How do we fight these things?"

"We don't," Nisra said. "We dodge them!"

The ground quaked again, as the freshly dispatched corpses rose, and more stumbled out of the tower.

***

"Mara, please give me back the staff," Levin said.

Mara's mouth curled into a cold, cruel smile.

"Levin, you do know how to amuse a girl."

"Just give it back to me and we can go home."

"Home? Mara said. "Look around you. The tower we stand on is dwarfed by some of the others we can see just from here. Do you have any idea how many people live in these towers? More importantly, can you imagine how many dead are buried here? The army I can raise here is astonishing. I'm not going home, Levin. I am home."

"You know I can't let you do this," Levin said.

Mara held the staff out, her green eyes fading to a dark scarlet. "Are you sure?"

Levin nodded.

The clouds over Mara's head swirled. Flashes of ruby red lightning streaked from the sky, and the crystal in the staff pulsed with a fiery red light.

"Goodbye, Levin!"

Levin squeezed his fist with a powerful sudden motion, pulverizing the crystal he was holding.

Mara's eyes went wide as flashes of red lightning struck the staff. The crystal on the staff exploded in a crimson flash, hurling Mara off the tower.

As the staff exploded into shards and splinters, a wave of barely visible light red energy emanated from the tower. As it rippled outwards, the wave shut down the constructs and the undead warrior collapsed to the ground, lifeless.

The wave shattered the mirror, reducing it to dust and the sky returned to its normal color. The silence was visceral for a moment.

***

Nisra and Bardok sat on the ground, sharing a skin of wine as Levin emerged from the tower.

"Did you get it?" Bardok asked.

Levin shook his head. "It is gone, as is Mara. We will count this as a victory."

"So, the money?" Nisra asked.

"That, unfortunately will have to wait. The money is at home."

"Then, let's go home, wizard," Bardok said.

Levin pointed to where the mirror had been. "I am afraid that is not an option right now."

The sounds of loud wailing began to fill the air.

"So, what do we do?" Nisra asked.

"I will find a way, but it will take time."

"How much time?" Bardok asked.

Levin shrugged. "A year, maybe less. Maybe more. Probably more."

"Well, I guess that leaves us no choice," Bardok said, standing up. "Let's find a tavern."

"And then what?" Nisra asked.

"It'll fall into place from there. It always does," Bardok said.

Random Lines From That Wistful Memoir I Am Writing

As the years drag by, inexorably taking me closer to the grave than the cradle, the need to leave a mark, no matter how small it may be, on the world grows stronger by the hour. If one is a writer, then the need to make that mark by filling pages with thoughts of things past and observations of the here and now in the context of a life that has been lived, then a choice, perhaps the only choice, is to write a memoir to share those ideas with the world, and, in turn, plant one's flag on the hilltop of history. Anyway, here are some lines from my upcoming memoir, *Where Has All The Whimsy Gone?*

1. There's something about an old-school diner. The food is as honest as it is real. There's nothing pretentious about the menu. You know what you are ordering and, more often than not, you get what you expect. We'd all be better off if people were more like diners.

2. I have never dated a Melissa. I say that with neither pride nor regret. It's just a simple fact. I have never dated a Melissa.

3. You look back on life and you regret some of your choices, maybe a lot of them. But the choices you regret the most are the ones you never made. Maybe a couple of things you did in college too.

4. The day you choose to stop learning is the day you choose to die. This is also true of the day you decide to fight a bear.

5. You will look back at the many trips you have taken and realize that no matter how many fancy cruises you may have enjoyed, the ship that will have served you best is friendship. If you're lucky, that's one ship that will never give you a bad Norovirus.

6. Growing older is merely an ongoing process of watching your dreams die. Growing wiser is realizing that that's okay, and maybe even for the best. It'd be ridiculous to have that many astronauts out there, for crying out loud.

7. Before the internet, or at least before we carried it with us in our pockets - which is amazing and would appear to a younger version of me to be nothing less than sorcery – there was a time when it was okay not to know. I miss those days when it was normal to argue over trivial matters for hours on end. Those were sometimes the best discussions and fondest memories. Now anyone can tell you within seconds the name of Boz Scaggs third album. I feel we have lost something here. Because sometimes the journey matters more than the destination.

8. Summer days would linger for us then. We would revel in the sun and wander aimlessly for hours on end without feeling the cold, sterile air conditioned chill inside. Now we avoid the sun and the heat, and, in a way, we avoid life, trading a lack of sweat for a lack of adventure and wonder.

9. We used to know our neighbors. Now we don't. Unless they are on social media. But do we really know people there? A friend is not what a friend was.

10. One day you just wake up and realize that *Puff the Magic Dragon* is infinitely sad, and from that day on your life is never the same.

11. In the end, all your mistakes, all your setbacks, and all your failings are what make you who you are, and maybe just maybe, make you better. Being a billionaire fireman would have been cool, though.

Madridsburg Square

An hour can contain an eternity.

Dominick sat on a bench in the Madridsburg town square trying to avoid glancing at the clock set in a black metal sculpted column beside the walkway that led to the county courthouse. An empty pedestal that until recently held the statue of a Confederate general was on the other side of the path. "Five minutes. She'll be here in five minutes," Dominick thought as he tried to take a sip from the Styrofoam coffee cup he had bought from the Center Diner on the other side of the square an hour ago. The cup had been empty for a half hour, but it gave him something to do.

Because Madridsburg was a small town, Dominick and Kim went to the same schools growing up. They'd been friendly, but it wasn't until high school that they felt something more.

Kim played on the girls' basketball team since junior high, but didn't began to excel until she was a freshman at Madridsburg High School. Dominick was a running back for the Cougars. In eleventh grade, the yearbook named them "Mr. and Miss Star Athlete." The photo shoot was in the gym. Kim, who was an inch taller than Dominick, guarded him on the basketball court, while he pretended to dunk a football. The yearbook photographer got frustrated with them because they couldn't stop laughing.

After the session, Dominick asked Kim if she'd like to go out.

"I think that's a perfect idea," she said.

The minute hand stubbornly refused to move. He started to pick off small pieces of his cup as he looked across the square at the Magnolia Theater. The mismatched letters on the marquee announced that the theater was showing "Rise of Sk walker" and "Avengers Endgam3".

Their first date was at the Magnolia, an old brick building with two movie screens. Dominick had picked *The Ring*. During scary parts, Kim squeezed his hand, and he debated whether he should put his arm around her. At about the hallway mark, he did. Months later Kim confessed that she acted scared so he would do just that.

After the movie, they walked to Dominick's pickup truck. He made small talk, and she laughed and gave him a quick kiss. "It's time to get me home. I don't want that ghost girl to get me," she said.

"This has been nice," he said.

"Yes," she said. "It really has."

Dominick looked away from the empty oil-stained spot where his truck had been parked that night and back to the clock. Another minute ticked by.

They dated through senior year. College scouts watched Dominick. Kim had no interest in pursuing basketball beyond high school. She liked to write, and worked on the school newspaper. She was as good a writer as she was a basketball player, probably better.

Dominick got a scholarship to the University of Alabama, while Kim would head to the University of Memphis, about an hour away from Madridsburg.

Two nights before Dominick left for Tuscaloosa, he and Kim ate at Jaleen's in the square, half a block from the Magnolia.

They vowed to stay together. They'd call and email every day. Texting wasn't really a thing quite yet. They thought they meant it. After dinner, they kissed underneath Jaleen's red awning.

Dominick traced patterns into his cup with his fingernail as he looked at the now tattered and faded almost white awning on the space that had been Jaleen's. It was now a hardware store. Two minutes.

College held too many options and distractions for Dominick and Kim, and they were both too young to ignore them. They split up before the end of the second semester. It wasn't ugly and there were no tears or recriminations. But, as friendly as it had been, the two lost touch.

By senior year, Kim was engaged to another journalism student. The following year, she walked down the aisle a week before Tampa picked up Dominick in round seven of the NFL draft.

Kim moved to Nashville, where her husband had landed a job with the *Banner* while Kim freelanced.

Another year, and Dominick was Tampa's number two back. He opted not to settle down in a serious relationship. While playing on the field, he found it to be too much fun to play the field. During his second season, a dirty tackle destroyed Dominick's left leg and with it his career.

Within two years, Kim's marriage was also sidelined. She had started to get pieces published in magazines – regional at first, but a few national pieces later. Her husband had started to drink and that helped fuel his resentment and jealousy for her success. He was sarcastic and demeaning at times, and at other times he was emotionally withdrawn. She brought up the idea of divorce. He didn't disagree.

Kim's freelance work was not to the point where it would pay the bills, she moved back to Madridsburg. She continued to freelance while working part-time for *The Madridsburg Mail*, the local paper.

Dominick took a coaching job at a small middle Tennessee college. Three years later, his mother died. He came home to help with the estate. One afternoon, he delivered some documents to the probate attorney at the courthouse. As he left, he heard someone say, "Dominick?"

He turned and saw Kim.

"Kim is that you?" he asked walking towards her with a slight limp. She smiled and nodded.

They had coffee at the Center Diner and caught up. Before the check arrived, they knew they were back together. It was like they hadn't missed a beat.

Dominick looked at the diner. The building looked the same as it had back then. A new coat of the same color paint, maybe. He'd bought his coffee there an hour ago. Even the coffee tasted the same as it had years ago.

It was time, but she wasn't there.

They were married within the year and bought a house near the college where Dominick coached. Kim regularly drove to Madridsburg for work and to see her family. Kim and Dominick tried to have kids, but gave up after two heartbreaks. Although they both knew it, neither would admit the strain was driving them apart. There was no big fight and no screaming – just an imperceptibly slow drift.

Kim's desire to freelance waned, but she still worked for *The Madridsburg Mail*. She started to spend more time at the office. The editor, Michael Gaines, was ten years older than her and they had a strong connection. He was married to the daughter of the owner of a local car dealership. Neither Kim nor Michael was particularly happy at home, and they found a connection with each other that had been missing.

One night they were putting the paper to bed in Michael's office on the second floor of the old house in the square that had been converted into a newspaper years earlier. They were joking around and Michael kissed her. They both stopped laughing and there was a moment where a decision could have been made. They both decided to take a step back and determine which path they needed to take.

Kim told Dominick everything. It was just the one kiss, but she didn't know if it she wanted it to be more. She knew that Dominick and she were dealing with mixed emotions. She knew that they still loved each other, but maybe they both needed something else. Maybe they deserved it. She needed time to take a breath. Dominick agreed.

Dominick looked at the The Madridsburg Mail office across the square. The brown shutters to the office upstairs were closed. Dominick crushed the Styrofoam cup and dropped it on the patchy grass.

Kim moved in with her family, and told Michael she needed a break from the paper, and from him. She needed time to sort things out. Michael didn't argue. He let her know that, no matter what, she was welcome back at the paper anytime.

Kim and Dominick didn't talk for a while. They both had picked up their cell phones to text or call countless times, but made themselves stop. After two months, Kim texted Michael with a simple "Hi."

He called her, and they talked pleasantly and inconsequentially for a few minutes before Dominick asked, "Are we going to make this work or do we need to . . ."

"Let's meet Thursday at 5 outside the county courthouse. We can give each other a decision then," she said.

***

Michael glanced down at his cellphone. There were no messages and no calls. The time on the phone was a few minutes behind what the hands of the clock in the square showed. Giving her the benefit of the doubt, Kim was six minutes late when she arrived. Dominick stood as she walked towards him.

"No matter how this goes, can you forgive me?" she asked.

"There's nothing to forgive," he said.

She looked down.

"But, yes, if you need to hear that, I do," Dominick said.

"I'm sorry. You didn't deserve this," Kim said.

"Neither of us deserve to be where we are," he said. "We should have done the work."

"I've made a decision," she said.

They waited.

"Dominick, let's go home. If you want to," she said.

He took her hand and said, "I think that's a perfect idea."

They looked at each other, and knew that it really was.

Bisbee Abstract

After ten miles, Alan started to relax. Thirty miles later, he thought he'd gotten away with it. After another ten miles, all hell broke loose.

***

Before he deployed to Iraq the second time, Alan had a wife and a baby girl. When he returned, he had an ex and a daughter he rarely saw. He loved his daughter, but he didn't love the idea of having to negotiate with his ex to see her. He didn't want to see how she was being raised by another man who she'd call dad. He carried the hurt in his heart and her picture on his phone. Maybe over time he could handle the situation without anger or sorrow. But, that would take time, and until then his contact with his daughter was going to be limited.

His family was not the only change Alan faced when he returned home to Phoenix. His old job was gone; the company had shut down while he was deployed. It took him six months to start looking for work. He was passed over for dozens of jobs before he finally landed a security guard position at an art museum in Phoenix. He was hired to work the night shift, which included two patrolling officers and one guard monitoring the video cameras.

One of the other officers also supervised the night crew. Steve was a nice enough guy. He didn't give Alan too hard a time and didn't ask a lot of questions. Paul, the other patrol guard was a short, stocky fireplug of a man. When he learned that Alan was a veteran, he started referring to him as

"Captain America" with a mixture of sarcasm and satisfaction at his absolute degree of cleverness. For a while, Alan didn't speak much with Steve or Paul beyond what was necessary for the job, which wasn't a lot.

Kerns – Alan never learned his first name – manned the video cameras. He was an older guy, maybe in his late sixties. Kerns always greeted Alan with a wave as he limped in or out of the video room. He seemed pleasant enough.

About a month into the job, Paul approached Alan. "Hey, Captain America, Steve needs to see you."

Alan got nervous. Had he done something to get himself in trouble?

Paul saw the sense of panic washing over Alan's face and laughed. "If you get fired, I'll escort you out so you don't break any statues."

Alan met up with Steve in a portrait gallery.

"You needed me?" Alan asked him.

"You've been working here a minute," Steve said. "I think it's time we get to know each other. You want to meet me and Paul for breakfast after our shift? On me."

Alan agreed, and Steve gave him the name of a diner nearby.

Over coffee, Alan talked in general terms about his military service, and vented about his ex-wife and how much he missed seeing his daughter. Alan noticed Paul's tattoo of a flaming skull on his forearm, which he hadn't notice before because he had never seen either Steve or Paul without their ridiculous long sleeved uniform jackets.

"Nice ink. You weren't military, were you?"

"Hell no," Paul said before adding. "I just like the art. That okay with you?"

"How you doing with the job?" Steve asked, trying to keep the temperature down.

"It's okay," Alan said. "I mean I could use more money,

right?"

Steve and Paul exchanged glances. Paul nodded.

Steve looked around and leaned forward. "Alan, buddy, let's make some money."

"You willing to bend the rules, Captain?" Paul asked.

"I guess it depends. What for?" Alan asked.

"A bunch of money, dumbass," Paul said.

"What's a bunch?"

"How's a hundred-grand sound?" Steve asked.

"Does it involve killing anyone?" Alan asked with a nervous chuckle.

"Probably not," Paul said.

"No," Steve said firmly.

Paul laughed.

"I'm serious, Paul. No one gets hurt."

"I hear you, boss man," Paul said.

"I mean it."

Paul held up his hands. "No one gets hurt. Got it."

Alan picked up his phone and looked at the picture of his daughter. "What do we have to do?"

"That exhibit in B gallery, that abstract crap, it's leaving in two weeks," Steve said. "The museum staff will crate it up the day before, and the transport crew will arrive at 6:30 a.m. to move the works to a museum down in Tucson. Only thing is, we are going to move it before the transportation people get there."

"How are you going to do that?" Alan asked.

"It's not a big exhibit. There were like twelve crates when they unpacked the show," Steve said. "All we need is a moving truck."

"What are you going to do with it?"

"I know an art dealer down in Bisbee. There are a lot of rich jokers who visit Bisbee and pay too much money for art. Plus this guy's tapped into a network of people willing to pay a lot for art that isn't widely available on the legal market."

"I thought Bisbee was just an old copper mining town," Alan said.

"It was, but now it's got this whole art scene for rich hipsters to drop cash," Steve said. "My guy will give us a half a million for the whole collection. Cash. Your take would be a hundred thousand."

Alan paused and took a sip of coffee. He was thinking about it more than he should. "That math doesn't add up," Alan said.

"You've been here ten minutes. It's fair, Captain," Paul said.

"I don't know," Alan said.

"Okay, look, I can give you another twenty-five grand on the deal," Steve said.

Paul started to protest, but Steve cut him off. "Fair is fair, Paul."

Paul looked away and nodded.

"Won't they know we did it as soon as they find out the pieces are gone?" Alan asked.

"Don't worry about that part," Paul said. "Our shift ends at 5. When the next crew comes on, there's still going to be packed crates for the transport guys to take away."

"But, at some point they are going to open the crates and figure out what happened," Alan said.

"Yeah, well . . ." Paul started.

"Don't worry about that part," Steve said, cutting him off. "It's not your problem, okay?"

"What do you want me to do?" Alan asked.

"You're going to call in sick that night," Steve said. I'll have the truck waiting for you in town. You just pick it up around 3 a.m. and drive to the museum. We'll load the truck, and be out by 4. You and me will drive a few blocks away, and Paul will wait around for the shift change so that nothing looks weird. He'll meet up with us, and then we are Bisbee bound."

"What about Kerns?" Alan asked.

"I'll roofie him. By the time he wakes up, we'll be gone," Paul said.

"But what about the next shift?"

"There's not a new video monitor guy until the museum opens at 10. They'll just assume Kerns fell asleep on the job. Again," Paul said with a laugh.

"No one gets hurt," Steve said.

***

Paul called Alan the night before and told him a small white moving truck was parked a block from Alan's apartment. "It has a Death Valley bumper sticker. The keys are under the seat."

Before he put down the phone, Alan looked at a picture of his daughter. He thought about calling his ex, but decided against it. He tried to sleep, but after a few restless hours, he walked to the truck.

Alan found it where Paul said it would be. It was a beat up moving truck with a cab separate from the cargo bed in the rear. A roll down metal door was closed in the back. The truck had a brown and yellow Death Valley sticker was on the rear right bumper. Alan opened the cab and fished the keys on a rental company fob out from under the seat.

He climbed into the truck and put the keys in the ignition. He closed his eyes, took a deep breath and exhaled. He looked at his phone and nodded before turning the key.

***

Alan backed the truck to the museum's dock and the loading door rose. As he got out of the cab, Steve ducked under the metal door.

"Let's go," Steve said.

Alan walked into the loading bay and saw about a dozen crates in various sizes in the middle of the floor. Another stack was against the wall.

"Where's Paul?" Alan asked.

"Making sure Kerns doesn't put an early end to this situation. Come on, let's load these crates," Steve said, pointing to the crates in the middle of the room.

They moved the crates out to the dock and loaded the truck. They were almost done when they heard a muffled bang.

"What the hell was that?" Alan asked.

"A screw up. Come on, let's get these last two in the truck," Steve said.

As they put the last crate in the back of the truck, Paul ran onto the dock carrying a shotgun. His eyes were wide and wild.

"Let's go! Double time it, Cap!" Paul said, climbing into the back of the truck.

"I thought ..." Alan started.

"Yeah," Steve said slamming the rear roll down door to the truck, as Alan stood frozen in place.

"Move!" Steve shouted. "We don't have time right now."

Alan snapped out of it, and ran to the driver's side. He got in and cranked the engine, and drove them away from the museum.

***

They didn't speak for the first fifty miles, silently moving through sparse traffic as the desert sky transitioned from black to purple.

"Fifteen miles to Eloy," Steve said, looking at a green highway sign. "I'd hate to end up there."

Eloy housed four adjacent penal institutions, the Red Rock Correctional Center, the Eloy Detention Center, La Palma Correctional Facility and Saguro Correctional Facility. The facilities are far and away the largest employer in Eloy.

Alan didn't respond. He looked across the divided highway. The median was sand and scrubs. There wasn't much traffic heading northbound towards them. It was just one eighteen-wheeler and a couple of motorcycles a few hundred yards away. No cops. At least not yet.

"Look, buddy, I didn't know Paul was going to pull that crap, okay?" Alan said. "But it's over, right? Just think about the job. Think about the money."

"That's ..." Alan started as a shotgun blast erupted, blowing a hole through the thin metal wall separating the cab from the cargo bed. The slug missed Alan's head and smashed through the windshield. Paul stood unsteadily in the back, aiming the gun towards the cab.

Alan ducked and shouted profanities as the truck swerved off the road kicking up sand and mowing down small cacti. Paul staggered and fell to the cargo floor. Alan wrenched the wheel and got the truck back onto the blacktop.

Steve pulled a Beretta 9mm from his belt and pointed it though the hole as Paul regained his footing.

"Brake!" shouted Steve.

Alan slammed the brakes, causing the truck to skid. Paul stumbled forward as Steve fired three times. One round caught Paul in the throat.

"No one was supposed to get hurt!" Alan shouted.

"Yeah," said Steve, holding the gun. "Let's go!"

Alan floored the accelerator, and the truck heading back down the road.

The two motorcycles in the other lane passed, then veered across the highway, doubling back. The helmetless riders throttled the bikes and they split off, flanking the truck on both sides.

One rider pulled even with Steve, levelling a shotgun. Steve aimed the Beretta and fired, forgetting the window. Glass exploded. The biker squeezed the trigger, painting the inside of the cab and Alan with Steve's blood.

Alan swerved. The biker's second shot peppered the side of the truck, punching holes in the white metal passenger door.

The truck careened across the median. A car fishtailed as its tires screamed and smoked, missing a collision by a hair as Alan forced the truck back into the southbound lane.

The biker on Alans's side pulled up, firing his shotgun as Alan jerked the wheel, slamming the truck into the motorcycle. The biker flew into the air landing head first on the asphalt, breaking his neck, as the bike cartwheeled into the opposing lane.

The shotgun blast shredded the truck's front left tire. Alan lost control as the vehicle lurched and flipped onto its side. The moving truck slid nearly forty yards with a cacophony of screaming metal and sparks.

Steve's body fell across Alan's legs, pinning him in place. The pistol flipped across the seat near Alan's right hand. His left arm and leg burned with pain, and he smelled gasoline.

The remaining biker rode to the front of the truck. The fingers of Alan's right hand crabbed towards the Beretta as the biker walked to the truck and aimed the shotgun. The biker nodded and smiled.

Alan emptied the Beretta's magazine. One round struck the biker in the chest as he fired his shotgun high and wild. The biker collapsed on the highway, his red blood spreading across the black asphalt.

The smell of gasoline was stronger. Alan could taste it. His left arm was broken, there was no doubt of that. He thought his leg was too. He extricated himself from Steve's corpse, and hauled himself out of the cab through the shattered windshield. His entire left side was alive with pain as he stumbled onto the sand.

He heard sirens. They weren't that far off. A blue highway sign ten yards ahead announced that Red Rock Correctional Center and its sister facilities were ten miles away. He could picture it in his mind. Faded brick walls and small cells. Metal bars and despair.

Alan pulled out his phone and looked at his daughter's picture on the shattered screen. He dropped the phone and grabbed the shotgun beside the dead biker. The dead man was wearing a black leather jacket with a flaming skull patch that was the spitting image of the Paul's tattoo.

As the sirens grew louder, Alan limped to the road and faced the truck's underbelly. The air was thick with the acrid aroma of gasoline. Paul fired the shotgun at the leaking gas tank. Nothing happened. He licked his parched lips and fired again.

This time there was a spark. The massive explosion consumed Alan in a hellish orange fireball.

Burning debris littered the road and desert. The truck's bumper smoldered in the twisted, smoking wreckage. The bumper sticker was charred, leaving only a single readable word.

Death.

Questions Raised by *Piano Man*

Billy Joel's *de facto* theme song, *Piano Man*, raises a lot of questions. And it is high time someone had the courage to ask them, which is the very thing I am doing now:

1. How does one make love to a tonic and gin? Or any other beverage? It seems that it would be ungainly at best.

2. Who has ever used the phrase "I knew it complete"? Maybe it's the kind of thing some monk would have said in the 15th century, but it seems unlikely that some old guy in a bar would talk like that. Unless he was a time-travelling monk. But it feels like that would have at least been mentioned at some point in the song.

3. When the old man says he knew the song when he wore a younger man's clothes, does he simply mean he knew it when he was younger, or did he murder some guy, steal his clothes, and sing a sad and sweet song? Seriously, why does the old man talk in this affected manner? I am now concerned he may be a serial killing monk who travels through time claiming victims. Do not steal this idea.

4. Is John a good bartender? He doles out free drinks, which can't be good for business, right? John is going to get fired at some point.

5. Is John a good actor? Could he, indeed, be a movie star? Has he tried acting? Or does he just think that, on the strength of his ability to quickly light cigarettes and tell jokes he could be a movie star? Even if he can't get out of that place

(for whatever reason), he could try acting at some level, don't you think? Maybe take a class or do some community theater. Someone's always doing *Our Town*, and that's a big cast. If John's any good, he could get a part. I mean, probably not the narrator, but maybe something like Constable Warren. I bet John thinks he's too good for that.

6. What kind of politics is the waitress practicing? Is she Democrat, Republican, Libertarian, or perhaps Green Party? Should she be getting political in a bar? It seems like a good way to irritate customers and reduce tips.

7. Why are the businessmen getting stoned in the bar? Drunk, sure. But stoned? And they are doing it slowly. How? The whole situation seems sketchy, if you ask me.

8. Who is sharing a drink called loneliness. Is it just the businessmen? Or is the waitress also somehow involved? Is that wise? And is it actually better than drinking alone? Depends on the other businessmen, I suppose. In any case, the bar should make them each buy their own glass of loneliness. But, obviously, John probably wouldn't bother enforcing that rule. The guy just does not care about the bottom line. At all.

9. What the hell is a real estate novelist? Is it a whole genre? I've never seen that section at a book store. Maybe you have to go to some real niche shops. In any event, does real estate novelling actually eat up so much time that you can't find a wife? I think Paul just didn't really want to get married and uses his weird writing career as an excuse.

10. But then again, maybe that explains why Paul is talking to Davy, who conveniently for rhyming purposes, is in the Navy. I am a little troubled that Davy intends to remain in the navy until he dies. I appreciate his service, but, man, shouldn't he at least want to be able to retire at some point.

11. I understand why the microphone smells like a beer. As we've established, John gives Bill beers, so it's no wonder

that the mic smells of free beer. But how does a piano sound like a carnival? Is Bill just playing that clown song over and over again? You know the one. They always play it at circuses. If that's the case, I do not understand why the bar retains Bill. Unless it is a clown bar. Which would be awesome, but unlikely, as real estate novelists hate clowns.

12. Is it appropriate to tip musicians with bread? Maybe it is in a clown bar.

13. When the crowd asks Bill "Man, what are you doing here?" is it because he keeps playing that carnival song, and is not actually hired by the bar? If so, John really shouldn't give him free drinks.

The Equinox Pattern

"You've got the drums too loud, asshole," Joey Dahl said, glaring at the engineer through the glass separating the live room from the control booth.

Dahl was the front man for Equinox, a hair metal band that charted in 1985. Now they were lucky if they could get booked on the county fair circuit. Dahl and guitarist Cord Hammer were the only two remaining original band members. Bassist Manson Gein, who wrote most of the band's hits, had died in '86. The band limped along a few years after that, but a lot of fans felt that Equinox died with Gein.

The band brought in a series of replacement bass players. They were all good, but they weren't Manson.

Equinox was recording their first album since '91, the year their label dropped them. "It's nothing personal," their manager said in a conference call from his office in Los Angeles. "It's just a numbers thing. Don't sweat it, we'll get you guys something else, soon, okay?"

A month later, their manager dropped them. The agency sent a letter with the news. The letter was nothing personal at all. Two days after getting the letter, drummer Danny Hotts quit and joined another band.

Cord always blamed Joey for Gein's death. Which was fair, because Joey Dahl murdered Manson Gein.

***

The gig at New Orleans' Lakefront Arena was a good one. The crowd at the sold-out show was loud and had one hell of a time. The late-night party after the concert was off the charts. The usual backstage debauchery was an appetizer for an insane visit to the French Quarter and Bourbon Street. Once the band was recognized, which was almost instantly, they were mobbed by fans and would be groupies, which was par for the course for Equinox in the mid-eighties.

"We're the kings of Bourbon Street!" Dahl shouted, receiving affirming cheers and screams in return.

The boys made their way from bar to bar, picking up their companion (or companions) for the evening. At some point, Gein gave the band and their overworked security detail the slip.

Gein staggered back to the hotel around 9 a.m., about an hour before Equinox was supposed to board the bus to hit the road for their next show in Memphis. Gein moved slowly with a distant gaze. He didn't pay any attention to the people in the lobby who recognized him. He simply drifted through the hotel without acknowledging the world around him.

When the band members dragged themselves onto the bus, Gein did not speak to the other guys. He just went to his small cabin near the back of the tour bus.

"Manson must have had a hell of a night," Danny said, kicking back on one of the red leather couches in the front half of the bus, watching the road and lake water roll by outside the window.

"He looks like crap," Cord said. "Either he had a great night or a terrible one. Maybe both."

"I'll go talk to him," Dahl said, hauling himself to his feet.

Dahl made his way to the back of the bus and knocked on the faux wooden door of Gein's cabin. Gein didn't answer, and Dahl knocked again. This time Dahl heard some mumbling from inside and took that as an invitation to enter.

Gein was sitting bolt upright on the bed. He was staring straight ahead at the wall. The shade on the window was down.

"You okay, man?" Dahl asked.

"Yeah. Yeah, I'm good," Gein said, not looking at Dahl. "Where are we?"

"About an hour north of NOLA."

Gein nodded. "Where's the next stop?"

Dahl sat down in the black leather chair beside a table. A bottle of whisky and a half-full ashtray sat on top of the table.

"Dude, Memphis. We have a gig there tonight. Then Nashville. Then Louisville. After that, I forget."

"Memphis," Gein said with a hint of wistfulness. "I recorded there when I was with Kill Bomb in '81. Bones Baer's studio. He's a hell of a producer."

"Yeah. It was a good album," Dahl said.

The two sat in the cabin for a while, letting the dull roar of the road fill the air.

"Manson, you okay?" Dahl asked.

"I'm good. Better than I've ever been," Gein said, still not making eye contact with Dahl. "Last night changed me, man."

Dahl frowned. "What the hell happened?"

"I met a girl," Gein said.

"That's nothing new, bud," Dahl said.

"This one was different," Gein said, looking Dahl directly in the eyes. "This one opened the gate."

"What drugs did she give you?" Dahl asked with a laugh.

"The truth."

***

She wasn't the usual big-haired twenty-one-year-old (or so everyone pretended) blonde with a black t-shirt and ripped to hell tight jeans. She was older, maybe in her forties. Gein wouldn't have been able to describe her later, other than to say her dark eyes burned with intelligence, desire, and power.

Gein saw her across the room in a packed bar on Bourbon street. She smiled at him, and he approached her. The air seemed to hum with electricity as he got closer. "Hello darling," the woman said. "I'm going to give you something tonight, and you're going to give me a present in return. We are going to change the world."

Gein stood still, and the woman leaned in and kissed him. His waking memories ended in that instant.

He recalled being in a dream, but not asleep. In this waking dream, Gein was lying in a field, his head on the girl's lap. Above him was a starless deep yellow sky. Points of phosphorous-bright lights streaked through the sky. The woman sang to Gein while stroking his hair. There was no wind or noise other than the singing, which echoed in his head, caressing his brain.

"Your song is beautiful," he said to her.

"Don't just listen to it, darling," she said in a soothing soft voice. "Feel it. See it. Close your eyes."

Gein closed his eyes and took in a deep breath. He smiled contentedly and she began to sing again.

As she did, Gein saw patterns of yellow light dancing behind his closed eyelids. He began to shake, and his mouth curled into a rictus, baring his teeth. His hands clenched at the ground, tearing up chunks of dirt and grass.

"You see it now, don't you baby?" the woman said.

"Yes," whispered Gein.

"But do you really, truly see it?"

"Yes," Gein said, louder.

"Will you remember?" she asked, the softness leaving her voice.

"Yes!" Gein said, his voice raising.

"Will you give it to the world?" she said, her voice becoming harsh and commanding.

"Yes!" Gein said.

"Will you do it in service of me?"

"Yes!" Gein shouted.

"You are mine and so is this world. Sleep."

Manson Gein woke up alone on the ground between two vaults in the Saint Louis Cemetery No. 1. His head was pounding. He stood up and instinctively reached into his pocket. There was a sheet of paper torn from a spiral notebook. Gein looked at the page and saw the words. The patterns were there.

"I am yours. This world is yours," Gein said as he started to stumble back to the hotel.

***

"Truth? What do you mean she gave you truth? Sounds like some new age crap, dude," Dahl said.

"She gave me a song, Joey. We will record it. We must record it. It's the most important song there ever was."

"We don't do important, buddy. We do kick ass," Dahl said, reaching over to grab the bottle on the table. It was early to be drinking, but, hell, he didn't drive the bus.

As Dahl took a swig from the bottle, Gein handed him the paper. "Take a look at this."

Dahl set down the bottle and looked at the paper. It was filled with random words and symbols written in blue ink in a hand that was far too precise for the mélange of nonsense on the page.

"Dude, this makes no sense," Dahl said.

"It will when you see the pattern," Gein said, nodding.

Dahl looked at the paper, shaking his head. "This is bullshit, Manson."

"Look. And listen," Gein said.

Gein started humming something that didn't sound like anything Equinox had ever played. It had an otherworldly quality that Dahl had never heard anywhere, much less from Gein. Dahl looked at the paper, and the light in the room dimmed. The words on the page seemed to move. Some changed colors, fading from blue to a faint jaundiced yellow before intensifying to a neon yellow. Lines formed between the words and symbols, and they floated above the page, swirling and rotating.

Dahl gasped and dropped the paper. He looked up and locked eyes with Gein, whose eyes were now yellow.

"You see it, don't you," Gein asked, pulling a large bone-cased folding knife out of his pocket.

"Yeah. I see it."

Gein smiled. He unfolded the knife then held his arms out wide, the blade extended in his right hand.

Dahl stood slowly and grabbed the whisky bottle. Gein looked and him and said in a dull voice, "We are hers. The world is hers."

Dahl smashed the bottle over Gein's head. The glass shattered and Gein collapsed to the bed without a sound. Dahl watched as Gein's body twitched and as the blood flowed, soaking into the bed.

He bent down and picked up the paper. The words and symbols were all in blue. He folded the paper and put it in his pocket, before walking out of Gein's cabin.

"He's dead!" Dahl shouted. "He tried to kill me! Oh God!"

The bus pulled over and Dahl told everyone that he had been talking to Gein, and that he was acting weird. "He attacked me with that knife out of nowhere," Dahl said. "I didn't think, I just hit him with the bottle. I was just trying to stop him. I didn't mean to . . . it was an accident."

Deputies from a nearby small parish in near the Mississippi border arrived shortly. Dahl was taken in. By the end of the day, a team of attorneys from the label made it to him, and by the next day a few strategic donations made sure that everyone was convinced that Dahl's story made sense and that no charges were pressed. The public story was that Manson Gein died in a freak accident after a night of excessive exuberance.

The band cancelled the remainder of the tour, and the members all made public statements about the evils of excess and the tragedy of losing a bandmate and, indeed, a friend.

For the most part, the public bought the story. Cord Hammer never did.

Joey Dahl locked the paper Gein had given him away in his home safe. He managed to lock the memories of it away in a vault inside his brain. Within a week of the incident, he simply forgot what happened. He believed the story that the publicists had spun. He didn't think about the paper again for decades.

After a six-month mourning period, the band got back together and tried to replace Manson Gein. No one could, and the audiences knew it. Equinox's genre was fading as it was. Manson Gein's death just made Equinox one of the earlier casualties of the end of an era.

The band continued to tour to increasingly smaller venues. Cord's relationship with Joey Dahl had never been great. After Gein's death, it was strictly professional. It was, as their manager would tell them, nothing personal. Outside of rehearsal and performances Dahl and Cord did not communicate.

And after the label dropped them, there was no communication at all.

Two years after Equinox was dropped by their label, Joey Dahl had a dream.

He was walking through a grassy field, a yellow sky above him. In the middle of the field were two chairs, one elevated on a mound above the other. Sitting in the lower chair was Manson Gein, wearing a black hooded cloak. In the taller chair sat a woman in a long black ceremonial robe. She wore a dull yellow crown and held a scepter of the same color. She grinned at Dahl while staring at him with eyes that burned into him.

As Dahl approached, he saw the chairs were covered with elaborate carvings of strange symbols that he recognized, but did not know from where.

"Manson, is that you?" Dahl asked.

Gein nodded, looking at him with blazing yellow eyes.

"Manson, where are we?"

"Darling, your friend cannot speak. He is missing something, aren't you?"

Gein nodded again.

"Show him," the woman said in a harsh voice.

Gein opened his mouth, showing that his tongue and rotted and shriveled to a black, useless stub.

"What the hell?" Dahl asked.

"He gave you a gift, and you have not used it," the woman said. "You have silenced his voice. Do you know how much pain that causes him?"

Dahl looked at Gein. Tears streamed down his cheeks, and he screamed. A guttural noise filled with regret and pain filled the air.

"See how you make your friend suffer?" the woman asked.

"What do I need to do?"

"Retrieve and share his gift. That is all," she said. "Do it for him. Do it for me."

"I will," Dahl said.

"Go," she said.

Dahl woke up and walked downstairs to his home office. He opened the floor safe and shuffled through the contents until he found the paper Gein had given him on the bus. He looked at the symbols and words, and felt a jolt of electricity course through him. He saw the pattern. He saw the song, and he grabbed a notebook. He suddenly had a handful of songs in him. As he wrote them, he could almost feel Gein's hand moving his. By morning, he had written five songs that were better than any Equinox had ever released.

For the first time in years, Dahl picked up the phone and called Cord Hammer. After an awkward exchange of courteous but skeptical pleasantries, Dahl said, "Cord, we've got an album in us. I've got at least one killer tune."

By the end of the conversation, Cord agreed to look at the songs. Dahl sent him a copy of the five songs he had written the night before. A couple of hours later, Cord called Dahl back.

"These are damn good, Joey," Cord said. "I haven't seen anything like this since you . . . we lost Manson."

"I'd like to record them," Dahl said.

"You rent the space, and I'm in. "

Two weeks later, Dahl and Cord met at a small recording studio in L.A. Dahl arranged for some session musicians to play bass and drums.

Jordan, a heavyset twenty-four-year-old sat in front of a monitor. Cord was lying down on a couch that had been ratty for longer than the kid had been alive. The rest of the band had split at 11:30, three hours earlier.

"You've got the drums too loud, asshole," Dahl shouted from the recording room behind the glass.

"Sorry Dahl is such a prick, Jordan. He thinks Equinox is still a thing."

"As long as you keep paying hourly, Equinox can be a thing, and he can call me an asshole."

Jordan adjusted levels, and Dahl grunted approval as he held the headphones to his ears. Dahl laid down the vocals in one take. His voice was not as strong as it had been when

Equinox was in rotation on MTV.

Dahl ripped off the headphones and walked into the control room. He sat in the torn recliner next to the couch. "That sucked."

"It's fine. We should have five solid songs," Cord said.

"Cord, I want to do one more tonight," Dahl said. "I found some lyrics by Manson. Stuff we never recorded. I can do the vocals if you can just play for me. We can add in the other shit later."

"How do you have a new song by Manson?"

"He gave it to me the night he died."

"Why the hell are you just now mentioning this, Joey?" Cord said.

"Do you want to see it or not?"

After a pause during which Cord couldn't decide whether his anger or curiosity was greater, he looked at Dahl. Curiosity won.

"Let me see it," Cord said.

Dahl opened his bag and pulled out the faded page of notebook paper that Gein had given him. He showed Cord the sheet.

"Is this a joke? This is garbage, Joey."

Dahl snatched the sheet back and rummaged through his bag. "Grab your guitar," he said.

Cord sighed and stood up. He picked up his electric guitar. "Just roll on whatever we do, Jordan. This won't take long."

Dahl walked into the recording room and put the sheet on a black metal music stand and slipped on his headphones. When Cord was in place and jacked in, Dahl hummed the tune he'd heard over three decades earlier. "Just play that."

"Whatever, man," Cord said, and started to play. The tune was easy enough, but sounded strange. There was an airy quality to the music. Cord didn't understand it, but he knew it felt right.

Dahl stared at the words on the paper. The music from Cord's guitar filled his ears. Dahl took a deep breath, and then the words and symbols on the page began to move and change color, from the blue ink to dull yellow, to glaringly bright yellow. The words spun and twisted above the page.

The pattern was there.

Dahl took a deep breath and started singing in a voice that was as strong as it had been during the Reagan administration. Cord played like a kid with something to prove, and not an old man who barely gave a damn.

A few minutes later, the song ended, and silence hung in the air. Joey and Cord pulled off their headphones. Dahl turned to Cord, and they both grinned, baring their teeth at each other. They both screamed the same deep lamenting cry that Dahl had heard from Gein in his dream.

Dahl grabbed his mic stand and swung it at Cord, who raised his guitar. The heavy metal base of the stand shattered the guitar. Dahl swung again, striking Cord on the temple. Cord collapsed to the floor. Dahl screamed 'We are yours!" as he bashed Cord's head in, painting the studio walls with blood and bone and brains.

Dahl dropped the stand and doubled over, breathing heavily.

Jordan opened the door from the control room and walked in.

Jordan opened his mouth and said in a voice that wasn't his, "See the pattern?" Jordan looked down at Joey with yellow eyes.

"Yeah. I see it. You are hers. I am hers. The world is hers."

Dahl fell to his knees and raised his arms.

Jordan punched Dahl in the face, smashing his nose. The singer didn't fight back. Blood flowed from his broken nose. Dahl looked up at Jordan with a grin on his face. "Hers," he said.

Jordan grabbed Dahl and slammed him against the glass window, knocking over the music stand which clattered across the floor. Jordan pulled Dahl back and slammed Dahl's head against the glass, sending spider webbed cracks through the window. Jordan pulled Dahl back and then rammed his head through the window. The glass exploded, shredding Dahl's face and neck. Blood geysered from Dahl's carotid arteries, painting the control panel in a wet crimson. Dahl twitched, and died.

Jordan looked around the recording room, his yellow eyes burning with power. He laughed in a harsh, deep voice. He picked up a shard of glass from the window that was lying on the ground beside Cord's body. Without hesitation, he slit his wrists with the glass. Blood pumped out of his arms, and he collapsed to the ground. The paper with the lyrics lay beside him. He picked up the paper in his bloody hands. He closed his yellow eyes. When his eyes opened, they were brown. Jordan started to cry, but he was too weak to do much else. He looked to his hand, and the piece of paper was gone. Less than a minute later, so was he.

The next morning, a young engineer discovered the three bodies. He managed to call 911 before he threw up his breakfast wrap. When the police arrived, they conducted a crime scene investigation. Their initial assumption was that this was a messed-up murder-suicide, probably brought on by drugs, alcohol, or some combination thereof. The investigators asked for a copy of anything that had been recorded the night before. The engineer downloaded the files to a thumb drive and gave it to the police, who promised they would only use it for the investigation.

After they left, he listened to the tracks. The first few were solid, but when he played the last one, his eyes went wide. With a grin on his face, he uploaded the song and labelled it "Equinox's Last Song." Within an hour, the news broke about Dahl and Hammer's violent deaths, and soon social media was buzzing that Dahl and Cord's recording from that night was available online.

It wasn't long before everyone could see the pattern, and the world was hers.

ABOUT THE AUTHOR

Joe Leibovich is an attorney, writer, podcaster, and former stand-up comedian and improvisational performer and director. In addition to this book, Joe is the author of *Too Fat for Europe*. His various projects can be found at *www.howlingmonkeyradio.com*.